A SECOND LOOK

Hannah Matus

A SECOND LOOK

Hannah Matus

TUGHRA
BOOKS
New Jersey

ISBN: 978-1-59784-946-3

Ebook: 978-1-59784-981-4

Published by Tughra Books

335 Clifton Ave.

Clifton, NJ, 07011, USA

www.tughrabooks.com

Library of Congress Cataloging-in-Publication Data

Names: Matus, Hannah, author.

Title: A second look / Hannah Matus.

Description: Clifton, New Jersey : Tughra Books, [2022]

Identifiers: LCCN 2021049348 (print) | LCCN 2021049349 (ebook) | ISBN 9781597849463 (paperback) | ISBN 9781597849814 (ebook)

Subjects: LCGFT: Romance fiction. | Novels.

Classification: LCC PS3613.A8733 S43 2022 (print) | LCC PS3613.A8733 (ebook) | DDC 813/.6--dc23/eng/20211008

LC record available at https://lccn.loc.gov/2021049348

LC ebook record available at https://lccn.loc.gov/2021049349

For my parents, who taught and encouraged me to reach for the stars.

For my husband, who aids me in the pursuit of my goals with the same fervor as his own.

For Ms. Shamsa, who handed me my first copy of Pride and Prejudice *and instilled in me a love of reading.*

For Salley, who makes sure I get out of my cave for regular outings and buoys me with the force of her positivity in life.

For my kids, for whom I started writing before they were even born, and all of my amazing and brilliant nieces and nephews.

For Bushra and Allyson for patiently reading and commenting on my first draft, and Kadi for always encouraging me, and Ameina for always being a constant source of joy, and for everyone who has always supported me.

And, first and foremost, as with everything, for the sake of Allah (SWT). May He accept it and forgive me any mistakes I made or anything wrong I have done or written. Ameen.

CHAPTER ONE

Maryam B. updated her status.

Hadith of the Day: A reminder for us young people to lower our gazes when looking at the opposite gender.

The Prophet Muhammad (PBUH) said,

"The first look is for you while the second is against you."

LeedyaMinLeebya commented on Maryam B's post.

Uh oh. Looks like our youth are in trouble.

~

Nothing brings about chaos in a family more certainly than preparations for the attendance of a wedding. Especially in a family of five young adult girls.

"Mama, Kawthar took the gold necklace you were going to let me borrow," Leedya complained. Elizza rolled her eyes as she pinned her hijab to cover her chest, under which it didn't matter if she wore a necklace or not—no one would be able to see it. Her younger sister Leedya, on the other hand, was trying out a new turban style for her hijab tutorial Instagram channel and needed some bling to offset the bareness of her neck—or so she said.

"They can't make me go," Maryam pouted. She was concerned that the wedding was mixed, i.e. not separated according to gender, but as it was the daughter of their father's oldest friend getting married, in an uncharacteristic show of firmness, their father insisted they all put in an appearance.

"None of my friends' parents would even *let* them go to a mixed wedding." Her arms folded across her chest as she leaned uselessly against the wall, making no effort whatsoever to get ready. Between her and Leedya, Elizza mused, they'd never make it.

"Look," Elizza said, patting her sister's shoulder, giving up pinning her hijab for the moment. Clearly it wasn't urgent. "Just—cover yourself as best as you can. And since you're just doing it to obey your parent, Allah will forgive you." Maryam pouted some more, then opened her mouth to retort with her superior knowledge of *sharia*, no doubt, before being interrupted by Leedya, who popped in from the hallway to rummage through her oldest sister Jana's closet for some alternative jewelry options.

"I'm pretty sure you're not supposed to reject invitations…in Islam. I heard that once." Maryam just glared, before stomping out of the room after muttering that she needed to get dressed.

"Leedya, you have at least ten times as much jewelry as I do," Jana protested. Leedya ignored her, exiting the room grasping at least five different necklaces to try. Elizza resumed pinning her hijab before turning to her sister, who was staring at her open closet, at a loss.

"Let's get you sorted, now."

***

Twenty minutes later, all the girls but Maryam were assembled in the foyer ready to set off.

"Where is that girl?" Leedya demanded, impatient to be off now that she had perfected her own look.

"Leedya," Umm ul'Banaat said, eyeing her daughter critically, "You are wearing too much makeup. And Elizza, you need to put some on. It *is* a wedding." Leedya rolled her eyes. Elizza said nothing. "Not you, Jana. You look beautiful, as always. Just the right amount."

"There's nothing Maryam can *possibly* be wearing that would take that long for her to put on," Leedya said. "*Mary!*" she screamed, hoping to infuriate her with the hated nickname. That appeared to work, because seconds later they heard her footfall on its descent down the stairs. Elizza turned and opened the door so they could all begin to file out of it. Leedya squealed.

"Oh my God, are you *kidding* me, Maryam?" Elizza's heart sank as she turned around and got a look at Maryam. Not because she objected to her wardrobe choice at all, but because she could predict the upcoming scene with a certainty. Maryam was wearing a black abaya, a black scarf wrapped around her hair. On top of her scarf was a niqab that obscured her face with a small open space for her eyes to peak through.

"Mary quite contrary," Kawthar said with a laugh. Leedya huffed, took a final look at Maryam, and sat down on the stairs, staring mulishly at the open door.

"There's no way I'm going with her wearing *that*," she said.

"Yeah, no way," Kawthar, Leedya's faithful companion, added. "It's embarrassing! Like, who brought the ninja to the wedding?" Their mother took note of Leedya's expression and turned on her other daughter.

"*Haiya* Maryam, *nihaha!*" Hurry up Maryam, take it off, she spat, out of patience with the scene. The other sisters took note of their mother's irritability and turned on Maryam as well.

The thing was, no one in the family was really aware of how much they indulged Leedya. She was just the youngest, always had been. By the time Leedya came around, their mother had enough older daughters to feel comfortable passing on the bulk of this one's care to them—and the emotional, spiritual, and educational development as well. By the age of five, Leedya had it worked out that all she had to do to get what she wanted, if her sisters refused to give in, was to bring the matter to her mother's attention. Their mother who, happy to have the "hard part" of child rearing over with by the age of 27 (mainly the birthing, breastfeeding, and potty training), was pretty much done being inconvenienced by her children and felt the time had come to focus on her own affairs and interests—which were, mainly, attending social events and gossiping.

So, the older sisters were very much accustomed to indulging, or heavily compromising what they thought was good for, Leedya at such a very young age that by the ages of 25, 23, 20, and 18, they hardly even noticed they were doing it.

Consequently, after receiving silent glances of "not it" from both Jana and Kawthar, it fell to Elizza to turn to her sister Maryam and say,

"Why don't you put on some sunglasses instead?" she suggested softly. "You aren't even wearing makeup."

"You're turning against me too?"

"Please, *habibti*," Elizza tried again, softening her tone. "Baba's been waiting for us for almost an hour in the car. He's going to have an aneurysm if we don't join him soon." Not that their father, strictly speaking, was the type to stress over such a small matter as lost time—surely he'd gotten over that by now as the father of five young adult females. Elizza really suspected that he fled to the car so early to escape the madness in the house. Still, she was ready to say almost anything to get them all moving.

Maryam took one long, tortured sigh and removed her niqab, exchanging it for the pair of sunglasses Elizza frantically pulled out of her purse, afraid Maryam would change her mind. Maryam made a show of it, taking a full minute to make the simple exchange, after which she made sure to walk out the door first, as if she'd been ready all along and not co-star of the drama that held them all up in the first place.

Not that their father noticed her come to the car first, looking all superior. They opened the passenger door of the car to find him reclined back in the driver's seat, his glasses a sneeze away from slipping off of his face, the gray suit he wore that doubled as his work suit wrinkling slowly. In short, he had fallen peacefully sleep.

Chapter Two

Abu l'Banaat and Abu Linda are celebrating 10 years of friendship on Facebook!

See their memories.

~

The sisters and their parents filed into the hotel, making their way toward the entrance of the banquet hall with the other 50% of the wedding guests who were showing up fashionably late. As for the other half, 15% showed up on time, 20% timed their entrance to be closest to when the food would be served, and 15% showed up at random intervals between other events to pop their faces in to exhibit their attendance before quietly slipping out.

They looked around the hall as the crowd made their slow pilgrimage through the doors to eventually disseminate as people played the Arab wedding musical chairs esque game to find seats. It was a lavishly decorated wedding, as Arab weddings typically were. The very end of the hall boasted a large stage decorated by two matching throne-like chairs in silver and blue with what seemed to be an entire greenhouse full of flowers arranged in the pattern of a mosaic against a lit backdrop. The tables were decorated with crystal vases boasting precisely matching flowers. Elizza did not know the names of many flowers, but she identified lilies, roses, lavender. It was beautiful—and typically extravagant. An ice sculpture bearing the names of the bride and groom, Linda and Walid, was slowly melting at the side of the stage. The tables were arranged to circle a dance floor in the middle of the room, where people were already assembled in the hopes that the DJ would take the hint and play something they could dance to so they could pass the time more quickly until the food arrived. Maryam eyed them all with distaste, thinking of the indignity she was currently suffering, having to witness coed dancing.

"We'll sit near the back," Elizza reassured Maryam in a low voice. Leedya turned around to glare.

"God, Maryam, just take those stupid sunglasses off. We look like we're leading in our blind sister." Kawthar snickered. Maryam's shoulders stiffened, but she didn't take off her sunglasses. Leedya sure knew how to make an insult hit home.

Elizza sighed inwardly. Maryam was obviously different than her other sisters, but alike in some ways too, notably their shared trait of stubbornness. For Elizza, faith was uncomplicated. She tried to be her best and do her best in every facet of her life, doing things according to Islamic guidelines, knowing she could always improve. She tried to dress modestly by sticking to knee-length shirts and baggy pants or skirts, knowing she could do more in the future.

She tried not to be judgmental of others. With her family, she couldn't afford to be. They were a good example of a spectrum of religiosity, with Leedya representing the more liberal end and Maryam holding on firmly to a more conservative outlook. The rest of them fell more or less in the middle. Elizza would give her opinion on matters of religion if asked, but never felt comfortable correcting or imposing it on others.

Elizza often thought that what made Maryam difficult to deal with wasn't her stance on things, which was often the most rigid and restrictive interpretation possible, but her insistence that she was right and everyone else was wrong—and how she constantly harangued everyone that they should all follow her way of doing things or they'd end up in an unpleasant place for all of eternity. In other words, she was somewhat of a downer. Not very pleasant at parties. Refused to go to ones with music unless her father made her go for the sake of etiquette (or so he said—the real reason was probably so he could have the house to himself for once and have a break from all of the women who normally inhabited it for a few sacred, glorious hours). She had a quick witted sense of humor and fierce loyalty to those closest to her, but no one could see it because her every other sentence was giving out unsought advice on *fiqh* and serving her daily share of "enjoining good and forbidding evil." She had very little tact.

Sibling placement, though, had been particularly hard on Maryam, who was born smack in the middle of two pairs who got along just fine. She didn't fit in with either pair well, but got stuck with the harsher younger two as a result of coming up just short of senior enough. She probably would have been better off sharing a room with the older, more sympathetic pair during those critical years of adolescence, but when the two bedrooms were to be divvied up between the five sisters, Jana and Elizza had just reached the critical years of their own adolescence, and though Jana probably would have given into Maryam's pleas not to be left alone with Things 1 and 2—as she called them—Elizza was not mature enough or nice enough to be denied her right as an older sibling to have more space for her things. She was also beginning to learn the value of privacy and keeping a confidence with her older, closed-mouthed sister.

Consequently, Maryam was left to fend for herself as best as she could, and her defense mechanisms only worsened over time. Her life goal unconsciously became to try to differentiate herself as much as she possibly could from her youngest siblings. Thus finding herself at the polar opposite end of the *sharia* spectrum.

Elizza found a table with enough empty chairs at it near the back to fit their family and secured it quickly, hoping her sister would brush off Leedya's meanness. Two chairs were reserved via the placement of a purse on top of one and a man's coat draped over the other.

It was often difficult for guests to sort out seating at a mixed wedding. Did the men go find seating with other men? Was each family supposed to find enough places for all their members at a table? Seating was rarely ever assigned at Arab mixed weddings, because you could never expect everyone who showed up to actually RSVP—or for those who RSVP'd to actually show up. Most times, you had to play it by ear. At some events, the guests were more in favor of gender segregation at tables and sat accordingly, with mixed gender tables being in the minority. At others, it was difficult for the more stringently religious, particularly those strict about gender segregation, to find seating at all, because most tables did have men and women who were not related sitting in close proximity to one another. Elizza eyed the man's coat dubiously, praying that the man who ultimately showed up at the table was old enough for Maryam not to make an issue of it. For herself, she figured that having their father at the table with them should be enough deterrence against the nefarious intentions of any bachelors' intent on catching the eye of a naïve young lady at a mixed wedding. She smiled at the thought.

And then commenced her family's wedding arrival ritual. Everyone scanned the room for acquaintances, with the exception of their father, who she knew was scanning the room to see how far along the meal preparations had gotten. Their mother was looking for the elite Libyan crowd. Their father's close friend Abu Linda, a connection forged in iron during their years as students at the same university, was *not* Libyan, but Palestinian [The very one to coin Abu and Umm ul'Banaat's nicknames, in fact—calling someone Umm or Abu anything was decidedly *not* a Libyan thing, but it was such a catchy and funny name (Father and Mother of "the Girls") that the Libyans found themselves using it too.]. Still, the friend met enough Libyans through Abu l'Banaat over the years to be able to include a substantial number of them when sending out invitations for his only daughter's wedding. They would mostly be seated together at the same tables, Elizza knew.

Libyan communities, like other communities built around the culture of the country from which the first generation immigrated, could be very cliquish. They probably should have been noticed as a family upon their arrival and brought by one of the Libyan ladies to sit near them. However, some families operated on the theory of association that sorted people into categories: the people that matter, and the people that don't. Umm and Abu l'Banaat's placement between these two categories was fluid.

Now, had Umm ul'Banaat married more advantageously, she would have loved to follow this theory of association herself. She thought, when her husband mentioned having a job at a college when he came to ask for her, that she was marrying a prestigious and socially middle class man who could and would associate with the upper echelons of the Libyan middle class, by default. She didn't understand the distinctions between tenured university professor and community college instructor, at the time.

However, the more fixed her husband became in the community, the more gradually the other families started to court his company and that of his wife. He garnered a sort of status as being one of the older and more fixed families in the community, having lived there for longer than many of the other families. But there was still that something that kept the richer families from too hearty an association; he was *only* a community college teacher, after all. He never had nor would ever be able to keep up with them as they bought their Lexuses and large houses, would never be able to reciprocate their hospitality as lavishly. So they never made it on the VIP list when it came to that particular and exclusive segment of the Libyan community.

And unfortunately for Abu l'Banaat, it was precisely this list that his wife craved to be on. She had her two goals in life—one was getting her five girls advantageously married. The other was to gain entrée as a permanent member of the elite of their small Libyan community—to be invited to all events, to be included as part of every dinner party that mattered, and for people to seek after her approval of the things that they did in their lives. In short, she wanted to be an arbiter of taste.

The second goal, she hoped, would be aided by the first—or vice versa, come to think of it.

Her daughters had different opinions about their mother's ambitions and the plans she made toward realizing them. Jana was ambivalent. She did not resist too much because, at the age of 25, she too was starting to get worried about her unmarried state. She did not possess the strength of character to not inherit her mother's worries for her.

Jana also scanned the room for acquaintances, but as an introvert, she got bored more quickly than the others and relied upon Elizza to let her know if anyone truly interesting, or a close friend, showed up.

Elizza quietly resisted her mother's schemes and matchmaking plans. They invariably led to embarrassment for her in the end, and her mother's disappointment in her second oldest daughter seemed to intensify each occasion she had to tell her mother "no" about some random guy who came to ask for her—who, thus far, were mainly Libyan natives (who either still lived in Libya or lacked permanent resident status in the United States) whom she could never be entirely certain weren't just trying to get a green card. Elizza scanned the room, and her eyes lit upon two tables side by side full of Libyans. Her friend Shayla, Shayla's younger sister Maariyah, and their parents were seated at one. Elizza slid over the faces of a few other community fixtures before noticing a young man she'd never seen before, handsome, well-dressed in a black suit and an unremarkable tie. He wore his beard close-shaven, had dark brown moppish curls and dark unsmiling eyes that contrasted with his whimsical hair. Shayla caught her gaze and danced her eyebrows at Elizza, having caught the direction of her stare. Shayla would fill her in on who the newcomer was. A few seconds later, however, she saw her mother make her way over to the table, pulling her husband along behind her. Looks like her mother would be the first to fill them all in.

***

But not before the other two guests that reserved seats at their table arrived to claim their seats, coming directly from speaking with the occupants of the pair of Libyan tables. The sisters lifted their heads, almost all in unison (with the exception of Maryam, who stifled the objection she was instinctually about to make), as they noticed a tall young man approach the chair holding the man's coat. He was dark and handsome, with impeccably groomed, clean lines shaping a beard cut so short it was almost nonexistent, and thick black hair shaped as carefully as a rich man's landscaping in a style Elizza had recently noticed many soccer players wearing. He was also blessed with an athlete's slender but solid build. He pulled his chair back to join the table, but paused in the process of sitting, apparently distracted. The sisters looked in his direction, and caught the flushed face of their beautiful older sister.

And Jana was a sight to behold, for those unaccustomed to seeing her beautiful face everyday. She had clear, radiant skin that no makeup could emulate. Her eyes were a clear honey color, and the thickness of her eyelashes made them appear even more soulful. She had a head of wavy dark brown hair that cascaded down past her mid-back. Today, it was covered by her hijab, but she was no less beautiful for wearing it—the gray of her hijab only intensified the unique color of her eyes. She was the second tallest of her sisters

(Maryam had them all beat there), was slender but not overly so. In short, she was a dream. And with her face flushed, she looked like an innocent doe waiting for a hungry wolf to gobble her up.

No one was surprised that she had caught the man's eye. They all experienced their interest in the gentleman fading fast—even Maryam, though she would have staunchly denied it if accused—for who could compete with the angel of the family? And none of them would ever want to—they were all united in that at least, their fierce, protective love of their near-perfect, kind and gentle oldest sister. They all dropped their gazes in resignation, saving a tiny bit of their former interest in the man for the express purpose of monitoring just how far his admiration for Jana would take him down the marital path.

With that, the sisters were all more or less free to take note of the woman who sat down quietly beside him, and wonder if she was his wife, and subsequently notice that the man wore no ring. *Interesting.*

After taking a drink from his water glass, he got ahold of himself enough to glance at the rest of his companions at the table. He smiled good-naturedly in everyone's general direction, and opened his mouth to speak, biting out a quick,

"Assalaamu'alaikum. I'm Mohamed—"

"BenAli!" someone interrupted from behind him. The man with the moppish hair. "Come sit over by me. Two of the *Amu's* have to leave." And with that, Mohamed BenAli offered them all a kind but apologetic smile as he and his sister got up to collect their things. The sisters exhaled sighs of disappointment.

"Sorry we have to move, but come say hello to my sister later," he said, before walking away to join one of the other Libyan tables. After which statement, the sighs were exhaled in relief.

***

Kawthar and Leedya were enjoying themselves. After their own scans of the room, they located interesting quarries and, rather than approach or trade sweltering gazes with them, practiced the age-old art of studiously ignoring them, seeming to vastly enjoy each other's company, laughing uproariously at each other's comments and taking selfies and snaps for Leedya's various social media pages every few minutes to document the occasion. Maryam just sat, boredom in her posture (and written all over the part of her face that was visible), and waited for her food. Finally, a handful of waiters dispersed between the tables to collect the pieces of paper upon which the guests were supposed to indicate whether they wanted a chicken, lamb, or seafood dish.

"Sisters," the waiter said as he approached, addressing them as a fellow Muslim, waiting for their chatter to die down before resuming. "I need to get your protein orders. But the bride and groom wanted me to let everyone know before you choose that the chicken is not halal, so keep that in mind." His eyes lingered on Maryam before asking their father what his meat option would be.

"Wait," Maryam asked, cutting off her father. "What do you mean, 'not *halal?*'" Her eyebrows were contorted over the rim of her sunglasses, picturing a chicken/pork meat mixture polluting everyone's plates, deceiving them all.

"Not *halal*. But, *yaa'ni, mish haram*," he replied. Not technically *halal*, but, you know, not forbidden either. And then he winked. She blushed. Her sisters turned away to hide their smiles. Umm ul'Banaat came back to the table just in time. She put in her own order—"Lamb, of course," as if there shouldn't even be another option—and proceeded to deliver the news of the new arrival, barely waiting for the server to get out of earshot. Or, as it were, *two* new arrivals.

"Two young men, business partners," she said excitedly. She could barely contain herself. "No, not related to anyone we know," she responded to Leedya's question. "Shayla's father knew one of their father's in the past, before he passed away. Both Libyan. Well, the one with darker hair, Mohamed BenAli they said his name was, is half Palestinian, but his father is Libyan." Which, as far as most Libyans were concerned, made him Libyan.

"Single?" Kawthar asked. Her mother was waiting for that question.

"Yes!" she cried. "And wealthy too. I told you they were business partners. They own an international trade business. That's why they are here; they are going to be giving a course at the university this semester about business." Elizza perked up. She was getting her MBA at the local university. She bet she would run into them there. Her spring semester just got much more interesting.

***

Elizza followed the bride with her eyes as she walked away from the table she shared with her new husband and her family to grace the dance floor, and almost groaned as she saw her mother take note. She knew what was coming next.

Umm ul'Banaat made her move. She walked over to the bride's dinner table and surreptitiously pilfered her water goblet. If they drank from the glass right after the bride took a drink, she believed, the bride's good fortune finding a groom might rub onto her daughters, and she had five of them to dispense of. Jana in particular was getting a little old. Leedya pounced on her mother as soon as she reached the table, stealing the glass away and guzzling it as thirstily as if she had just finished running a 5k.

"You're gunna drink it all!" Kawthar squealed, prying the glass away from Leedya. Water sloshed over the side of the glass. She took a quick swig from the bride's cup before their mother snatched it away again, making her way toward Elizza, Jana, and Maryam's side of the table, handing it first to her eldest daughter. Jana took a dutiful, quiet sip. Before their mother could even turn in Maryam's direction, Maryam rolled her eyes, saying, "I'm not drinking that, Mama. You know it's *haram* to believe in that superstitious stuff, trusting in other than Allah—"

"Uskuti, Maryam," her mother said, cutting her off. *Be quiet.* "Makuntish nibi na'tihoolik, aslan." *I wasn't going to give it to you, anyway.* "I hope your *salafi* friends are going to find you a husband. You don't listen to anything I tell you." She turned her scornful eyes away from Maryam to land on her second-oldest, and second-least favorite, daughter, handing it to her almost as an afterthought, and walked away to find some other mothers to gossip with.

Elizza looked down at the goblet. She confirmed that her mother was not the first to do this as she took note of the collection of fingerprint stains from all the other hopeful single ladies, the pushy moms, and the maroon lipstick stain of the bride. The reflection of a nearby candle glittered across the surface of the quarter-cup that was still left of the supposedly lucky liquid. It more likely held a cess-pool of germs from at least a dozen different young ladies, Elizza thought wryly. She glanced at her mother to ascertain her back was turned—no need to rile her unnecessarily—and splashed it into a nearby plant.

***

Tarseen snorted, having watched the scene play out from a distance. BenAli eyed him oddly before saying, "What's that?" Tarseen looked up, shaking his head to clear it, and resumed his former conversation with his friend.

"If I knew this was going to be a mixed wedding," Tarseen said, "I wouldn't have come."

"I know," said his friend, with a pat on the back. "That's why I didn't tell you. But now that you're here, why don't you try to enjoy it?"

"It's kind of hard in a mixed environment, BenAli. Lowering your gaze gets kind of wearing after a while."

"The Prophet, *salla'Allahi alaihi wa salam,*" peace be upon him, BenAli said with emphasis, "said the first look is for you. So you can save yourself the eye strain."

"I don't think the first look excuse extends as long as five seconds."

"Don't be so literal," BenAli said. "I'm pretty sure it just means don't be a pervert." Tarseen raised a brow.

"Man, I wish I brought a pen and paper with me. I don't want to miss any of famous *hadith* scholar Mohamed BenAli's free in-depth analyses."

"Okay okay. I'm just telling you try to lighten up a little. You've been talking about possibly getting married for months now. How's that going to happen if you don't work up any interest towards any particular woman? You gonna let your aunt pick out your wife for you?"

"God no."

"Alright. Let me tell you who I'm finding out about for myself so you can back off." Oh God, Tarseen thought. Another one?

"See that girl sitting at that table to our right?" The table was uncomfortably close to where they were standing next to the bar (that was only serving water, teas, coffee and sodas for the day). "The one in the gray hijab. But I did hear that none of her sisters are married either. There's one sitting right next to her. Try working up an interest in her and we can be in-laws."

Tarseen's eyes involuntary followed the direction of BenAli's gaze back in the direction from which he'd just torn it, like a boomerang. And there it stayed, soaking in details. Olive skin. Thick lashes. Enormous dark eyes. He gazed at her until it drew her eyes to his face, like a magnet. Flushing slightly he glanced hastily away and shot his friend an angry look.

"No thanks. Look, stop wasting your time with me. Aren't you missing a *dabka* or something?"

BenAli smirked behind his glass of soda, throwing out a, "Oh yeah. That's my jam right there," before hopping onto the dance floor and joining the queue.

***

Elizza's face turned hot with embarrassment. No thanks? Based on nothing more than a cursory glance at her? She left the table to sit next to Shayla, Maariyah having recently vacated her seat to gossip with Kawthar and Leedya. They were showily, and loudly, all taking selfies close to the bridal stage. Extremely close to the dance floor, but not actually on it—as lenient as their father was most of the time, he would never allow them to dance in mixed company.

She stared at the dance floor to give her something to look at that would discourage Shayla from trying to talk much, trying to soothe her ruffled pride. Elizza had stopped listening to music the year before, having read some *hadith* and commentary indicating that it was best to avoid it. And she could see why, really, given the fact that most music these days centered on themes of fornication, drinking, and other no-nos for practicing Muslims. And she was never particularly into it, so it was not a hard thing to give up. But as the music blared through the speakers, the quick beat of a tabla, and she watched a large group of men and a few daring women move their bodies in the step, step, back, step, hop move of the dabka, she inwardly cursed the bride and groom for making this a mixed wedding. She dearly wanted to dance her nervous energy away. Not that she was letting the man's comment get to her, she told herself, but she felt alive and confident when she danced. Comfortable in her own skin. A girl could always use that feeling, and even more so after hearing herself assessed and dismissed by a virtual stranger.

But she didn't have that luxury, so Elizza had to try to find some other way to nurse her wounded pride. She thought with disappointment over the evening—it started out so auspiciously, but she felt the damper of the man's dismissive comment now—felt drab and unattractive, and embarrassed that she was not immune to the unfavorable opinions of others. She looked around for her father, hoping to catch his eye and signal to him that she, at least, was ready to go. Her father had a soft spot for her, out of all of his children. He would take note of her weariness and round the others up to leave. Another of the things he was strict about, in contrast with his normal easygoing manners. She found him conveniently near the exit, speaking to a young gentleman she didn't recognize. She stared at her father long enough to draw his gaze her way, nodding her head to one side to indicate they should leave. Her father nodded. His companion turned to look in her direction curiously and caught her gaze.

Intense green eyes looked in her direction and did not move away for some seconds. Elizza shivered involuntarily. The look was cool and assessing, and approving, she noted, as he smiled before looking away and resuming his conversation with her father. She looked away, too, feeling awkward and un-Islamic. She tried not to stare too hard at people of the opposite gender, no matter how attractive. Lowering your gaze wasn't just for men.

But she felt warmed inside, nonetheless. Maybe she needed that. Sometimes, she thought, your own self-esteem and inner confidence can hold you up against criticisms and disappointments. And sometimes, maybe you just need a smile from a handsome stranger.

CHAPTER THREE

Umm ul'Banaat liked a video by Libyan Mom Recipes, "Ahsan Bazeen kilayta" Best Bazeen I've ever eaten…

Umm ul'Banaat tagged Maryam B, LeedyaMinLeebya, ThatRiverInHeaven, LazyLizza, and Jana bint Leebee in a video by Libyan Mom Recipes, "Ahsan Bazeen kilayta" Best Bazeen I've ever eaten…

~

Following every social event, a detailed gameplay and analysis is quite necessary. So necessary, in fact, that if Umm ul'Banaat and her friends hadn't already made plans to meet the following Friday, they would have planned a get-together just for such a purpose. As it happens, Abu l'Banaat was hosting the annual dinner he held for the noble cause of feeding the starving local Libyan single men—young able-bodied men perfectly capable of cooking for themselves or providing themselves a meal, but hey, let's feel sorry for them because they don't have women to feed them the traditional food their spoiled arses were used to before they made the perfectly conscious decision to abandon their homelands for a new life and boundless opportunity in America.

As scheming as it seems for Abu l'Banaat to hold a dinner for the local singles, he really didn't do it for the sake of marrying off his daughters. In fact, the event was gender separated, as many events in that Libyan community tended to be, and unless a man and woman happened to be collecting their food at the same time, the two genders barely had any interaction whatsoever. No, their father did it for other, different reasons that had more to do with his days as a university student, his "glory days" as the girls liked to refer to them, than the benefit his daughters might glean from having all of the local singles collected in their house one evening a year. He was nostalgic for his life as a single, relatively attractive, young Libyan male. He also genuinely enjoyed the company of the younger men, finding much more in common with them than you would expect between men with at least a 30-year age gap. And he considered this dinner to be his consistent *sadaqah*, an act of charity that he kept up year after year to please Allah (SWT) and to accrue in his account of good deeds in the afterlife. Okay, he also did it to keep his wife happy, despite all the obstacles that existed to keep her daughters from actually running into a single man long enough to incite his interest. Still, Umm ul'Banaat had no qualms about single-handedly planning and cooking most of the food for the event, because at the very least, it was a great opportunity for the local single men to get to know her husband and find him genial enough to want him to be their father-in-law.

The house was full of the local Libyan matrons and a few of their older daughters. Some of the elite, rich Libyan crowd even showed their faces. Umm ul'Banaat reigned supreme on these occasions, getting the phone calls she craved from the elite Libyans, not because they suddenly decided to accept her into their crowd, but in hopes that she would invite them to the dinner her husband was hosting and thus their own daughters might have serendipitous meetings of their own. Of course, they could always host their own dinners, but with Umm ul'Banaat shouldering the bulk of the work and cost of these dinners, why should they bother? Their daughters could learn a thing or two about how to cook Libyan food, because really, who had the spare time to teach their daughters everything they needed to know how to make before marriage? And their daughters could do worse than learn how to cook from Umm ul'Banaat who, regardless of what else they thought of the woman, everyone regarded as an excellent cook.

Elizza watched as an elite Libyan specimen and her daughter walked in now, a family she did not know much about. She liked to observe Libyan mothers with their daughters. It was comforting to see her mother's idiosyncrasies reflected in other women. It reminded her not to be so judgmental - her mother was a product of the culture she grew up in.

Regardless of the pervasive Libyan culture, the mother-daughter relationship still presented a wide array of diversity, which is precisely why they were so entertaining to observe. There were mothers desperate for their daughters to get married, like her mother. But there were also the extremely prideful mothers who always seemed to have a daughter who used to be "at the top of her class in Libya." Elizza had heard so many girls were first in their classes it made her wonder how many schools there were in Libya. Some of them were fiercely protective of their daughters' university degrees. So much so that they almost seemed to discourage anyone from even thinking of letting their sons ask for them until they at least had bachelor's degrees under their belts. Some even went as far as claiming their daughters would finish medical school before they would entertain marriage offers. Elizza sometimes felt sorry for these girls; while she admired their mothers' dedication to their education, she often wondered if their mothers were living their unrealized dreams vicariously through their daughters, or if they were using their daughters' educations as a gateway to filter out the more "undesirable" category of man – i.e. the uneducated and lacking in finances. There were some who took marrying off their daughters to another level, whose conversations could not be veered very far away from discussions of whom had an eligible son of an age with her daughter and how to get ahold of him. But the category that Elizza looked at with the most envy was the mother who was very close to her daughter, and became her friend. They would dance together at parties. Exchange jokes over banquet tables. Once a girl asked Elizza if she knew of any new series on Netflix that were good because she and her mom were running out of things to watch. *What would it be like to have a mother like that?* she often wondered.

"Elizza," her mom barked, startling her out of her reverie. "Come watch the ladies put spices in the *usban*. You will need to learn it before you get married." She sighed sadly. She would never know.

***

The kitchen was a den of activity, everyone working on different parts of the meal to be served that evening. Large wooden bowls were scattered on every flat service that was available and contained the various ingredients that are used in virtually every Libyan dish—a bowl of parsley, diced tomatoes, fried onions, diced raw green onions, potatoes (fried diced pieces and raw sliced), diced lamb, chicken, and ground beef. *Hararaat,* a Libyan spice mixture, and cumin and turmeric and cayenne pepper were placed in smaller bowls for communal use. Some of the women formed a circle around an aluminum bowl with the ingredients to *usban,* a type of Libyan sausage stuffed with meat and rice. Elizza stood there long enough to be seen by her mother before escaping to help with something else. Umm ul'Banaat was hovering over the kitchen sink, cleaning the intestines to be used as the sausage lining. The younger girls were put to work rolling fried potatoes, onions and chicken into egg roll wrappers in a dish known as *bureek,* and rolling the semolina wheat flour into small balls of *cous cousi.* The Arabic stores did sell pre-made *cous cous,* but their mother was determined to teach her daughters the authentic methods of Libyan cooking that she lamented were being forgotten by the younger generation of Libyans, even those who lived there.

A just barely toddling little girl with a riot of dark curls and wide black eyes tumbled into the kitchen, fresh off of emptying the contents of their father's office drawer. Leedya picked her up just before she collided with one of the aluminum bowls holding ingredients. The little girl was so excited her legs kept moving even after lifted off of the floor, her mother nowhere to be found.

"Mama said no kids while cooking the food, but we'll make an exception for one as cute as you," she said.

Umm ul'Banaat strode over to playfully scold the little girl. "*Ya Shaytaana,*" she said. *Little female devil.* And pinched her cheek affectionately. "*Hoot alaiha!*" Which translates roughly to, put the evil eye protecting fish on her, she's too cute.

The little girl cried. Her mom materialized out of nowhere and folded her daughter into her arms, trying not to glare at her hostess.

"The new generation is raising them soft here," Umm ul'Banaat remarked.

***

For once, the topic of conversation among the older ladies and among their daughters was the same—the room was abuzz with speculation about the two newcomers. So far, they had eaten dinner in the homes of two Libyan families, Shayla's family, to Umm ul'Banaat's envy, and the home of one of the Libyan elites. The other Libyan matrons reported having their husbands call them to issue invitations, only to get summarily rejected.

Umm ul'Banaat was angry at her husband for refusing when she insisted that he invite the two for a private family dinner earlier that week.

"I am inviting them," he said with a smile. "They will be here on Friday, like the rest of them." On *Friday*, her daughters wouldn't have any special opportunities to be exhibited in front of the two gentlemen, she argued. But her husband just smiled and said, "I don't want to make it too difficult on you, *Hayati*. You will already have so much to prepare this week." But hearing the ladies discuss the rejections of their own invitations, Umm ul'Banaat felt a sense of relief that her husband hadn't tried. It was somewhat rude to reject an invitation to eat dinner at someone's house in Libyan culture, especially if you did not offer up a good reason as to why. It was seen as bad manners, a thinly veiled effort to avoid certain people's company. In this case, however, all of the bad manners were attributed to the man named Firas Tarseen. The one named Mohamed BenAli was friendly, outgoing, and eager to accept invitations from the local Libyans, if his friend didn't refuse on his behalf first.

Shayla nodded her head in agreement when hearing the ladies discuss the two men.

"Yeah, they only came to our house because BenAli accepted it. He also accepted the invitation from Amaima Sundus, too, but after that his friend kept making excuses for them. He seems sort of anti-social, from what I could tell."

"Don't forget rude," Elizza added, remembering his comment about her.

"Probably," Shayla agreed as she rolled another *bureek* into a triangle. "We didn't get much of an opportunity to find out anything about them. Mama had the table all prepared for everyone to sit together at the dining table, but Firas Tarseen saw the table and was like, 'Oh, we don't want to disturb your wife and daughters, we'll take our meals to the living room and eat on the floor.'" Leedya snickered.

"Sounds like Maryam," she said.

"Well, that's how all men *should* act when they get invited to dinner," Maryam said defensively. "It's best to keep the genders separated."

"Mama was sooo mad," Maariyah said, laughing. "She was cheated out of her marital schemes *and* had to try to eat dinner worried about what would happen to the living room carpet the whole time." They all looked expectantly at the shy young lady whose house BenAli and Tarseen had also graced with their presence. She blushed at the attention, and confirmed Shayla and Maariyah's account of the men's approach to eating dinner with the women of the house.

"BenAli did come into the kitchen to personally bring his plate," she added, blushing even redder. Kawthar and Leedya looked almost envious. Not because they didn't have his attention, but because they didn't have that story to relate.

"Don't pay any attention to her," Shayla said, as an aside to Elizza. "Actually, Firas Tarseen ended up leaving early to pray isha at the masjid and Mama set up all of the tea stuff on the kitchen table so he had to come back in the room and drink tea at the table. But he didn't show any interest in us," she added wistfully. "Instead, somehow the conversation landed on your family and we ended up telling him all about you guys."

"Anyone in particular he was asking about?" Elizza asked with a smile, already remembering his face when he saw Jana at the wedding.

"Jana, of course," she replied. "He asked my mom what she thought of your sister. Normally my mom hates saying anything nice about anyone else's daughters. Sees it as a competition or something and doesn't want us coming up short. But she freaking lovvesss Jana and couldn't bring herself to say anything bad about her. I could almost see BenAli falling in love with her by the second. It was kind of disgusting. I mean she's lovely and an angel but no one is as perfect as people are telling him she is."

"She comes pretty close though," Elizza said out of sibling loyalty. Jana was loved by all the Libyan moms, especially the ones with eligible sons. Elizza was not such a big hit. She got along great with everyone, but the moms looked at her with a sort of disapproval.

They couldn't quite put their finger on what exactly they disapproved of. They just had an instinct that this girl would give their son trouble if he was to marry her, and so they warned each other with subtle looks and some outright rude comments about her, to steer their sons away. They wanted someone *haadiya* for their sons. Elizza was still trying to tap down the exact Arabic to English translation of that word, but the general idea of it was quiet, shy, obedient. All she knew was, she was *not* it. Maybe she was not shy enough, so unlike her sister. Or she was too opinionated. Or the dresses she wore to parties were too mature looking for an unmarried girl to be wearing. And she was studying business, of all things. What did she think she was going to do with that degree? Starting businesses was for men.

She looked around to spot Jana, face beautifully pink from the activity of flitting around to help out her mother's friends as much as possible instead of sitting at the table gossiping with the other young girls and completing the least onerous activity their mothers would let them get away with. Yep, Elizza mused. An angel.

They heard a ring at the doorbell, and there was a collective scramble as everyone wondered who was at the door and if one of the young men mistook the time the dinner was supposed to start (they still had an hour until it officially started, and probably more like two hours before all the guests arrived). Jana was the first to hastily wrap a scarf around her head and an abaya around her short sleeves and patterned harem pants to go open the door a fraction to see who it was. Several seconds later, she ushered in a young woman she eventually introduced as Kareema BenAli, and the subsequent murmur in the room confirmed her to be BenAli's younger sister.

She was the same woman who came to the wedding with BenAli. Elizza did not remember much about her from the wedding. She was a very slender, tall young woman. She came in wearing a black abaya with matching hijab emblazoned with hundreds of crystals in a geometric design around the wrists, hem, and a larger version of the design on the center back. She took off a pair of expensive looking sunglasses when she walked into the kitchen, placing them neatly back into their case and into a pocket of her Prada purse. She stood on the threshold to the kitchen then, looking around, clearly at a loss where to sit or what to do.

"Oh, I forgot," Shayla said in a low voice. "My mom told BenAli to bring her along when he came here. She was sure your mom wouldn't mind."

"I thought he was just visiting here for a semester," Elizza remembered. "What's she doing here with him?"

"I guess she lives with him, so wherever he goes, she goes, too."

"I wonder if that trend will continue when he gets married," Elizza said, thinking, *if it does, it will make him an enormously less desirable husband.* Kareema was ushered over to where the younger women were sitting. Elizza put out her hand to shake it, ready to kiss her cheeks four times in the customary Libyan to Libyan greeting (Libyan to any other nationality—two or three…it varied), but she somehow found herself unable to do so. Kareema pulled herself awkwardly out of reach. Elizza stood there dumbly.

"Umm, I'm Elizza," she said, introducing herself. Kareema assessed her outfit, rumpled sweatpants and matching t-shirt, before saying, "Elizza? What an…interesting name," rather unkindly. She had no idea.

Elizza's name had been a source of contention between her mother and father in their second year of marriage. Elizza was actually named by her mother. After asking friends for suggestions on Muslim names that could pass for "American" from her friends, she liked the sound of it and stuck to her guns. In all fairness, she did not have to fight very hard for the name. Elizza was born within the first two years of her parents' marriage, after all, still the "honeymoon period" in some marriages. Any idiosyncrasies her husband noticed in her were indulgently attributed to her two pregnancies. Her husband's strongest objection to the name was that it sounded too close to one of the pair of pre-Islamic Jahiliyah Arab idol names mentioned and criticized in the Qur'an, *Al-Lat* and *El-Uzza*.

"My friends told me it means unique and noble. Allah knows that it is not our intention to copy Arab god names."

After Jana and Elizza, her mother got the rest of her Muslim but also American-sounding Muslim girl names, with the exception of Kawthar, who was named after her grandmother, who passed away around the time of Kawthar's birth.

Jana kindly found Kareema a chair from their father's office and sat Kareema at the table with the other young women. Kareema eyed their activity with distaste.

"Mohamed told me some women were arriving earlier than the men, at this time," she said. "He didn't mention why, though." She removed her hijab, uncovering her glossy, straightened, long black hair. Then she took out her Iphone, the latest model of course, and scrolled through her various social media pages. Umm ul'Banaat, having been updated as to the identity of their guest by the other mothers, strolled over to their table to give her *salaam*, all solicitousness and hospitality. Kareema shook their mother's hand lightly, but did not get up out of her seat.

"Yes, I will have some water," she responded when Umm ul'Banaat asked her if she would have something to drink. "With ice." Jana raced to get her a cup of ice water. Umm ul'Banaat's smile stayed fixed on her face.

"Do you know how to cook Libyan dishes?" Umm ul'Banaat asked her.

"No," she responded. "We had a maid when we lived in Libya, so…" Jana returned with the water and a plate of some of the food they already prepared. She placed it in her lap, and alternated nibbling her food, checking her phone, and taking sips of water, until dinner was finished. She stayed fixed in her spot, answering in monosyllables to the several girls and women who tried to ask her questions, and did not get up when the women and girls dispersed to place the food on trays, set out dishes and utensils, and do other things to prepare for the grand feast ahead of them, earning herself a reputation for being cold and unfriendly.

"The opposite of her brother," Elizza said in an aside to Jana.

"I'm sure she's just shy," Jana said. "She doesn't know any of us here. It would be hard for anyone to be comfortable being around so many women you don't know for the first time." Elizza said nothing. She didn't like the way Kareema seemed to make a pet of Jana, and there was a huge, discernible difference between the facial expressions of someone who is shy, and one who considers herself above her company.

***

The evening was a resounding success, as usual. All of the matrons complimented Umm ul'Banaat on her hosting prowess and gave her credit for everything turning out to be delicious, as the one who dictated the proportions and added most of the spices. Her daughters had some interesting accidental encounters with some of the young men, she noted with satisfaction. BenAli and Jana were getting second helpings at the same time at one point—or rather, BenAli was getting a second helping and Umm ul'Banaat suddenly needed her daughter to go get her a plate full of seconds. She didn't need to go spy on them, but knew deep in her heart that her daughter must have made even more of an impression on the young man, who by all accounts was already starting to ask other people leading questions about her.

Firas Tarseen actually deigned to put in an appearance, a fete the other Libyan ladies attributed to the reputation of her cooking. She managed to make Leedya and Kawthar sit down to take in a few lessons on flavoring food when cooked in large portions, Maryam managed to not say anything too annoying to her in front of her friends, and Abu l'Banaat and a few of his friends insisted on giving the ladies a break and washed all of the dishes. Yes, she was very satisfied.

***

Elizza couldn't sleep, and she was in denial as to why. She kept forcing herself to have other thoughts, thinking around the issue instead of confronting it head on as she should. But it was no use. She had to work it out, or she wouldn't get any sleep. And she loved her sleep.

She couldn't get the evening's scene out of her mind. Walking into the kitchen for seconds to see Jana and BenAli conveniently getting refills at the same time—and conveniently alone, saying nothing to each other as they picked up random food items with which to fill their plates as they practiced not making eye contact. And BenAli sliding past Jana, stopping before he left the room to stare at her as her back was turned to him, and then disappearing from the room like a ninja.

And Elizza's feeling of emptiness as she watched. She knew it wasn't envy, or jealousy. It was another type of selfish, unworthy feeling. The feeling that if her sister moved on—or when at this rate—where would that leave her? Only painfully, sorrowfully alone. The last particle in the vacuum before emptiness prevails.

Jana needed this in her life. To move on. To have someone value her for who she was. To love and appreciate her, make her the center of his world in the way she was never able to be as the oldest of five sisters. She really hoped that BenAli turned out to be that man, for her sister's sake.

But Elizza wasn't sure where that would leave her. She longed, too. Longed for someone to truly see her—not her beauty or education or outspokenness or anything else, but to see *her*.

She would do what Allah (SWT) commanded, be her best Muslim self, but she silently prayed for a partner to help her along the journey. Maybe she needed to do something tangible to get there? She woke up to pray *tahajjud*.

Chapter Four

LeedyaMinLeebya posted a video. Hey guys, check out my new video. I was gifted this amazing gauzy black face veil from @ReveilAll so I made a tutorial on doing a smoky eye with a twist, making your eyes really pop over the veil, with a contouring element to help your features shine through to advantage through the transparent fabric. Leave me a comment below and you can win a free sample of the shade of lipstick I apply at the end. And I want to send a special appreciative shout out to **Maryam B** for the inspiration. 😘

Maryam B commented on LeedyaMinLeebya's video. 🙂

~

The first day of spring semester arrived. Elizza had few classes that first day, but a very important meeting with her advisor to discuss what she needed to do to finish her business plan. She was due to graduate that semester and had a lot of work to do on her plan, her biggest graduation requirement. She had sent what she had written so far to her advisor to review during winter break. She sat across from him now, looking at him anxiously, waiting to get his advice.

"It's…good," he said at last. "You still have some holes to fill, however."

"Like what?"

"I couldn't say, exactly, not knowing much about the state of Libya right now. But you need to have it looked at by fresh eyes. You know, we have two visiting Libyan businessmen for the semester giving some classes and lectures."

"I've heard," she muttered.

"You could attend some of their talks, for a start. There's one coming up this Friday. I think you should go."

"Okay," she agreed.

***

Later that week, Elizza stared moodily into the flames of the fireplace she was sitting next to at the Panera on campus, lost in thought. Her plan still needed work, but he didn't know what to suggest? Typical advisor. She knew she should be reading over her plan and taking notes about what she could improve, but she didn't have the heart. She was exasperated. She wanted to go home, but it would be pointless going all the way home when the lecture started in a little over an hour.

She tried to think of something positive. Jana seemed to be radiating happiness. She'd never seen Jana so exuberant about anything before. It was an extremely good sign, even though it was too early to make the predictions her mother seemed at liberty to make.

Could this courtship be any weirder? Elizza always had trouble imagining just what "Islamic attraction" looked like before the guy asked the girl's father for permission to talk to her. How far in love could you get when you weren't supposed to really talk to people of the other gender outside of chaperoned settings, and weren't really supposed to look at people of the other gender, like, *ever*, and anytime two people of opposite genders were seen talking to each other in a communal setting, you could bet the entire assembly of people would be as rapt in attention to the conversation as either of the participants themselves could be.

And if anyone asked her to characterize in one word how Jana and BenAli fell in love—after their wedding (she earnestly hoped it would lead there)—she'd have to say "smiles." As far as she had seen, they had not spoken more than a few words in passing to each other. But, oh, there were plenty of smiles. She wondered if anyone else noticed. Their mother surely had. That had to be the reason behind her smugger than usual smile these days.

"Hey," a male voice said close to her, one she did not recognize. She looked up into green eyes in a handsome, tanned face, a face that she knew she'd seen somewhere (how could anyone forget such a face?) but couldn't remember where. "You're Abu l'Banaat's daughter, right?"

"One of them," she replied with a slight smile. "Hence the nickname."

"Yeah. I remember seeing you at the wedding. Linda's wedding," he seemed to feel the need to clarify. As if weddings grew on trees in this community. The mothers sure wish they did. "Her brother's one of my best friends. I talked to your dad for quite a bit. Cool guy. I was trying to get his recs on a good major or a good course schedule to take at the community college for an easy transfer to the university. He told me about some sessions they do monthly for hopeful transferees." She nodded distractedly, wondering about his background.

"So, George *Wi'am*, I take it you're not Libyan?"

"No," he said, smiling.

"Palestinian?"

"Close," he said. "Lebanese." She wondered if it would be rude to ask if he was Muslim.

"Yes, I'm Muslim," he said to her surprise. "Everyone always wonders. I could tell you were wondering, so I thought I would save you the trouble. My dad converted after my mom passed away. We actually lived in Libya for a while. But I moved away after my dad died."

"I am so sorry about your parents. May Allah have mercy on them." They drifted into silence. Elizza tried not to gaze too dreamily into his green eyes, knowing her younger sisters would embarrass themselves, and her, if they were near. In general, they were more overt about their crushes, but Elizza knew she had to come to terms with her own weakness. During the period of her adolescence, her burgeoning womanhood, high school and throughout college, her awareness of the other sex had been an involuntary thing that crept up on her unasked for and unwanted. She would come into contact with these guys, or boys really, who she really didn't even like all that much. She could discern the weakness in their characters in a heartbeat, see into the core of their insecurities with ease. Figure out what they were hungry for in life and discern their superficialities. And yet it was these guys who would make her palms moist with sweat when they approached, whose presence sucked the air out of her chest, whose offhand comments to her made her speechless and inarticulate. Not the top-of-the-class guy with his subtle opinions and depth of character, but the attractive, muscular idiot.

But that fact meant she was fortunate in her crushes—in a sense. Unfortunate in that she even had the disturbing unrequited feelings, but fortunate in the sense that her physical attraction to guys and her admiration for them as intellectual, good human beings never seemed to align. That discrepancy alone kept her safe. All the men she felt a physical pull towards were almost always unsuitable—for various reasons. Take her partner for an economics class she was paired with for an entire semester—supposedly at random, but she suspected her middle-aged female professor to be having fun with her partner arrangements, pairing the covered *hijabi* girl with the hottest guy in the class. Extremely attractive, athletic build, as she had come to realize was her preference. Athletic without being overly and intimidatingly muscular. Dreamy brown, wavy hair that he styled differently almost weekly. Even dreamier hazel eyes. Kind smile. Funny even, sometimes. But she knew he was full of himself. A little self-conscious in a blustering way that tried to hide it. A little stupid and simple in his opinions, as if he couldn't be bothered to contemplate things too deeply, possibly because a person that good looking rarely had to exert himself. She knew all of this about him. She even found it hard to like him at times, when he was blustering the hardest, and for *her* of all people. And yet, she couldn't help blushing when he'd catch her absentmindedly staring at his near physical perfection—those times when the second look got hazy and she was just so in awe she literally forgot not to stare. Or when he sat next to her as he had a habit of doing before they had to give a joint presentation. Or when he just spoke to her. But as awkward as she felt at these moments, she knew she was never in danger of falling into the types of mistakes that led some of her friends far away from identifying as Muslims, and some to have hasty abortions behind their parents' backs. Her feelings were always stabilized by her levelheaded consciousness. And those moments when she felt a real, intellectual, empathetic connection with a guy, she never felt the pull of physical attraction strong enough to put her in danger. And the aforementioned classmate was not Muslim—her crushes rarely were, oddly—which presented even another barrier. So many obstacles in the way she could only count as a blessing—Allah's (SWT) way of protecting her against the type of temptation that would cause a rift between her and her family and drive a wrench into all of her plans.

She tried not to center her life around dreaming of relationships or marriage or guys—there was more to life. More that she had to offer the world than merely being some guy's wife. She had hopes, dreams, ambitions. "Marriage is half of our religion," Maryam liked to remark, but without showing much interest in being a wife herself. Sure, Elizza thought, but I'm not even done refining the other half yet.

For all of this, though, she did harbor a secret hope, a deeply buried belief that she was almost ashamed of. That she would recognize the soul of the one Allah (SWT) created as the pair to her own, when those feelings of physical attraction and emotional connection would converge, and the ultimate package showed up on her doorstep, to see and claim *only* her.

She felt the familiar stirrings of attraction tickling her belly now, in George's presence, the detection rendering her silent with dismay. She looked up at him helplessly, wracking her brain for something charming to say.

To her relief, a blond girl from one of her classes approached, stopping next to her table for a chat.

"Hey Elizza," she said. "Great job on the business plan presentation." The girl paused to glance at George, waiting for an introduction.

"Umm, George, this is my classmate," she said, forgetting her name. She was introducing someone she barely knew to someone else she barely knew. How fun.

"I thought it was a really ingenious plan. Will really help the people in… umm.. I'm sorry, what country?"

"Libya," Elizza supplied.

"Oh yes. The one next to Syria, right?" Elizza and George shared a smile.

"One continent over. The one next to Egypt." If her father were here, he'd obligingly draw a map, she thought, her thoughts drifting off as George took over the conversation. The girl appeared to be having a conversation with Elizza, but her glance kept sliding over to George. It eventually drew his notice, and he turned the full effect of his charm over to her direction. *Giving me a much needed break,* Elizza thought.

"I'm going to refill my coffee," Elizza said, unnecessarily. The two were happy to carry on the conversation without her. Happier probably. When she returned to her laptop and bag, to her relief, they were both gone.

***

Elizza sat next to her father and Jana in the small room designated for the business lecture. She was surprised a few moments earlier to run into her father, who explained that he was attending the lecture in support of his fellow Libyans, having heard about it the night of the dinner they hosted a few days before. He tried to get Leedya, Kawthar and Maryam to join, but as the first two could not envision running into any particularly interesting male specimens at the lecture, and the latter thought there might be too *many* men at the lecture, they were not interested. The room held about 25 people total, not bad attendance for a business lecture. Elizza had attended more sparsely attended ones in the past.

The men's talk did not last long. They had a presentation prepared about how the political stability in a country, or instability, impacts business, and offered strategies for how to overcome those setbacks. Soon they opened themselves up to a question-and-answer session.

"Is your bottom line or overhead more impacted when you're doing business in a country that is politically unstable?" Elizza asked, referring her question to BenAli. She did not want to flatter Tarseen by directing her question to him. But BenAli was gazing absentmindedly at Jana, and forgot that he was in front of a room full of people, ready to answer their questions. Tarseen nudged him to attention.

"Sorry, what was that? It was difficult to hear..." Elizza raised an eyebrow at him before repeating her question. The same distant expression came over his face, and he looked in danger of asking her to repeat herself a second time, before Tarseen intervened.

"Actually, I'll take this one," he said, shooting an annoyed glance at his friend. He turned to look directly at Elizza, giving her an indulgent look before opening his mouth to answer. "The question was worded a little oddly, but I think I get what you are asking."

"You know what," she said, cutting him off, flushing angrily at his manner. "Never mind. I'll send my question in an email, or something." He stared at her for a second as she resumed her seat before asking the audience if there were any more questions.

Elizza counted the seconds down until the talk was officially over, standing up to make a beeline for the door before her father even put on his jacket.

"Elizza!" someone called as she walked past. She sighed in exasperation. Her advisor, standing next to Firas Tarseen. "So glad you came over here to talk to Mr. Tarseen. That was an impressive talk. I'm sure he wouldn't mind answering your business plan questions."

"Oh, I... I didn't walk over here to ask questions."

"That's all right. You're both standing here now. I'm sure he wouldn't mind." She glanced across her advisor to gauge Tarseen's expression. His face was unreadable, except that he looked uncomfortable being put on the spot, and looked everywhere but at her.

"I don't mind," he said politely, at last. "Ask away." She just shook her head.

"I have to get going, but thanks. Like I said, I'll shoot you an email." And with that, she made her escape. She wouldn't be shooting him anything in future if she could help it.

CHAPTER FIVE

www.google.com

Typing…

E
L
I
Z
Z
A

B
E
N
T
A
L
E
B

Did you mean ELIZZA BENTALIB?

~

U nfortunately, in this novel we don't get many opportunities to peer inside the brain of the elusive Firas Tarseen, so let's make the most of it.

We find him sitting peacefully in his car, a Qur'an CD playing Imam Al- Ghamdi's recitation of *Surah Al-Baqarah*, trying to review his memorization. To his chagrin, he is finding it hard to focus. His mind keeps drifting off in contemplation of some other thoughts. Thoughts related to a certain interesting female. Trying to figure out why exactly he was drawn to her. Perhaps it was her crazy family that enhanced her virtues in a sort of beguiling illusion. The bulk of her family bouncing around the place like they were caught in a whirlwind, flitting here and there like bees collecting nectar from every passing flower, and then there she was—calm and steady, like a rock. Solid. The eye of the storm. An anchor. The Queen Bee. And then, once he looked in her direction—actually allowed himself a real, lingering look, those eyes—

The sound of the driver's side back door opening jolts him out of his thoughts.

Kareema. She's not going to wait for her brother before she joins me in the car? he thinks. She locks eyes he can only adequately describe as carnivorous with him in the rearview mirror once she secures the door.

Okay, that's cool. Except it's not.

"BenAli's coming in a minute," she explains. "He's in the bathroom." Then she adds, "It's freezing outside." *Some excuse. Bet you guys have heat in your hallway though.*

But he says nothing. He moves to turn up the volume of his CD to cover the awkward silence, but she again leaps into conversation.

"That was some wedding the other day," she says. Silence. "Did you enjoy it?"

"Not really," he replies. "I only went because BenAli dragged me there."

"Yes, it wasn't to my taste either. Too much…intermingling."

"Yeesss…" he answers, drawing out the word, reluctant to agree with her about anything—aligning with her in any way whatsoever seemed like a bad idea—but being unable to resist inflecting his voice to encourage her to ponder the irony of her statement. He glances in the mirror again to see. She, apparently, hadn't moved her gaze away from his. *Over her head,* he thinks, disappointed.

"I was trying to figure out who all the Libyan families were and talk to them, but every five seconds I seemed to run into one of those annoying *Banaat,* so I thought it was safer to just stay in one place."

Ghamdi finishes his recitation of Ayat al Kursi. Tarseen flips the power off resignedly. He would at least respect the Qur'an and keep her gossip from intermingling with the sacred *ayat.* A second later, though, he regrets it as she continues to speak, encouraged by the silence.

"It's so funny, everyone thinks they're the most beautiful family of girls in the area and yet not one of them is married yet. Must be some reason for that, for sure. The younger ones are like, afraid to end up unmarried like their sisters and on the prowl." She gurgles out a laugh.

"It's definitely becoming a *fitnah* these days, the lack of decorum between young men and women, when their parents don't want them to get married early." Her face looks confused, but she nods her head solemnly anyway.

"Absolutely." And then she continues to talk, but Tarseen allows himself the luxury of allowing his mind to drift, trying to nod at sufficient enough intervals to be polite.

Did she hear me? he wonders. The few times he'd caught the girl's eye (he hadn't gotten around to getting her name- it probably wasn't a good idea to publicly show that much interest), at the wedding and a few days ago at his lecture, she glanced away almost instantly. He liked that. It showed a level of modesty some of her other sisters seemed to lack. He pictured her face as it looked the other day at the lecture, the way she flushed with embarrassment when he offered to answer her question, like she was uncomfortable with the attention. A rather beautiful face.

He needed to collect some more information about her. Not that he had plans to do anything with that information, or that he was urgently looking to get married at this point, but it would be interesting to know more about her. What was she like? Did she have a job? Was she studying?

Was she already engaged? he wonders, his mood darkening all of a sudden at the thought.

"And the younger one is some sort of Insta Famous *hijabi*," Kareema was saying. "I can't even imagine the chaos in that house." She paused for a second, looking out the car door before continuing. "And between you and me, BenAli is seriously thinking of asking for the older one. That would make them my in-laws!" She shuddered dramatically. "And then he laughed and said he was going to try to get you to marry her sister- the annoying opinionated one, of all people. He's ridiculous sometimes. Like she has any redeeming qualities."

"Except her eyes," he murmured unthinkingly, and then stopped at her dumbfounded expression. Of all the stupid things to say, to Kareema of all people. The passenger side door opens to cut off the awkward silence.

"Kareema?" BenAli calls, poking his head into the car to peer into the back seat, finding her. "Oh, there you are. I was looking for you. I thought you'd wait in the hall...?" He shoots an apologetic glance at Tarseen. Tarseen just smiles back, actually thankful to have the direction of his thoughts cut short. Thinking of the whirlwind that surrounded her, his heart races uneasily. *Yes. It's probably best to steer clear.*

Chapter Six

Mohamed BenAli updated his relationship status.

It's complicated.

~

"Ooh, look at this," Leedya squealed after coming back inside from checking the mail. She trekked out to the mailbox to see what they received daily, always in expectation of a package of free goods from companies asking her to promote their products. "A letter from Kareema BenAli, for Jana." She handed it to her sister, sitting quietly at the breakfast table eating her eggs and halal turkey bacon. Jana placed it beside her plate and continued to eat.

"Ugh," Leedya groaned, impatient. "How you can just sit it there and not open it...?" She grabbed it and unceremoniously ripped through the envelope, pulling out what looked like an invitation of some sort. "We're invited to... some BenAli relation's wedding. Ooh that sounds fun!" she said, but then her face darkened. "Well, looks like we are decidedly *not* all invited to this wedding." She opened the card so the rest of her sisters could get a look at the page.

RSVP: _____ *of* __1__ *guests will attend.*

"Rude," Kawthar chimed in, chomping on her cereal. Otherwise, she appeared unconcerned.

"It's not surprising, really," Elizza added. Jana looked disappointed.

"She probably couldn't invite so many people to her relation's wedding last minute," Jana said finally.

"Well, then she didn't have to invite any of us at all now, did she?" Elizza replied. "Don't get offended. Look, they're rude, plain and simple. That doesn't mean their brother is that way, or he wouldn't even be likeable. You'll just have your work cut out for you with those in-laws."

"Elizza, I wish you wouldn't say stuff like that. You're making a lot of assumptions. And anyway, Kareema is always kind to me."

"Yeah well, only the biggest jerk could be mean to you. You're so gentle and nice. You're like the ideal wife and daughter and sister-in-law, all in one. They know you'll never complain about anything."

"Please," Jana insisted. If she was firm about anything, it was keeping people from talking badly about others.

"Okay, think what you want. I'm sure she just needs someone to drive up there with her, not wanting to go alone." And sure enough, within the next hour, Kareema called Jana.

"We can drive up together," she suggested. "BenAli can't go early because he has to give some lectures, and I can't *possibly* wait so long to go up there. I need at least three hours before the wedding to get ready."

***

At noon on Friday, the girls saw their sister off. No one envied her solo invitation. Kareema showed up in a rented Mercedes, asking Jana to drive the three hours so she could paint her nails along the way. Elizza pitied her sister in advance for having to endure the scent of acetone the entire drive up.

"You don't have to go," Elizza told her as she helped her pack her bag.

"But I want to," Jana said, somewhat embarrassed. "Kareema needs someone to go with. She's paying for the hotel room; it's attached to the banquet hall. And it sounds fun." She didn't mention the brother. She *never* mentioned the brother. Elizza sent her a knowing smile.

Kareema bid farewell to Elizza before leaving with Jana.

"Sorry, I would ask you to go too, but it was so last minute, and my cousin…" she trailed off.

"Don't mention it," Elizza replied. "Jana gets bad glare at night," she added, "so it might not be the best idea to let her drive when it gets dark out."

***

Jana and her friend were supposed to drive back the next day, to be home sometime in the afternoon, after attending the "morning after" brunch of *aseeda* and *sphinz*, a Libyan tradition. But instead, Elizza got a text from her sister around noon.

Salaam Elizza, not coming back today. I'm a little sick and not feeling up to the drive. We're going to stay another day so I can rest. Please tell Mama.

Elizza sighed and let her family in on the bad news. Her mother didn't seem too concerned, however, and seemed to think her illness might move things further along with BenAli, saying something along the lines of, "men can't resist vulnerable females." The illness itself, she refused to think of as an illness at all.

"Your sister got '*ain* at the wedding," she said—she was deathly afraid of the evil eye. "See, that's why I always tell you, *yaa banaat*, to read the prayers on yourselves whenever you go to events like that."

***

Elizza decided to give Jana the day to get better before she'd worry. But when evening fell, and she hadn't gotten a follow-up text from Jana, she started to get concerned. She did not want Jana to be stuck with strangers if she really felt ill—especially with someone like Kareema. When Jana responded to her inquiry as to how she was feeling now with a sick emoji, Elizza made up her mind. She would just stay with her until she felt better. She packed a bag of clothes and some of her study materials in case she had downtime, placing her laptop on top of her clothes but unable to find her charger.

"Leedya probably borrowed it," she mumbled. Leedya's Mac charger recently gave out on her, and even though she practically brought in her own source of income, she was too cheap to buy a new one and was constantly recharging hers using Elizza's. Elizza walked upstairs and opened the door to the room Leedya shared with Kawthar and Maryam. Leedya was in the midst of recording an Instagram video, her face lit up with enthusiasm, her words buoyed by her natural charm.

There was really only one way that Elizza could think of to comprehensively describe her sister—she epitomized joy. That was her primary goal in life, despite her three oldest sisters' suggestions that there were other purposes in life. But she couldn't see why a Muslim girl couldn't pursue pure joy if she wanted to. Why did everything have to be *haram*? She didn't, in fact, believe that all the things people said were *haram really* were. She did what anyone ever asked of her. She prayed. She wore hijab, and covered her lovely mass of raven curls, even though she knew she looked glorious without it. She couldn't help the fact that she was still pretty wearing it. In fact, her sisters could take a leaf out of her book when it came to *hijabi* style. Just ask her 30,000+ Instagram followers. Some days, Elizza walked out of the house looking shabby. And there was really no hope for Maryam. They'd never get husbands dressed like that, and hijab did not have to equal unattractive, or frumpy.

Leedya had a mainstream, popular kind of beauty. She wasn't stick thin, but rather on the curvy side. She kept her waist small relative to her hips by sheer will—and the waist-training corset sent to her for free for promoting it by Elegantly Skinny. She was busty, but not as busty as the bra sent to her by Bustier Moi made her look. Her eyes were impossibly wide and big, made even more so by the free makeup sent to her by various makeup companies with contour collections, and that made her hijab styles and videos more popular than they ought to have been. She could pull off any style, any color, because her eyes were so prominent that they stole the show away from her hijab. So this girl promoting different ways to don modest religious outerwear ended up looking more beautiful by virtue of her scarf styles, and garnering more attention, male and female, than she ever would have received if she didn't wear one.

Leedya was talking to her mirror and wrapping a scarf around her head on top of a flesh colored underscarf she had obscuring her hair.

"And you all know the Turban style is really hot right now," she was saying, "but I've been experimenting with what I call the Gypsy style. I find it's not as bulky and you can really do a lot with the two extra pieces that are left when you're done wrapping." Elizza watched as she demonstrated different ways to wear the extra flaps of her headscarf. Not a practice run then, but a hijab tutorial. Leedya

wouldn't interrupt her video to tell her where it was now. Impatient-
ly she headed to Leedya's desk to rummage through and around it.
Maybe she'd get lucky.

"... also shows the lobes of your ears like the Turban style, which
is great. These earrings I'm wearing now are from Francesca's. I'll
post a link to them in the comments section once I'm done here and
Elizza you JUST walked into the video frame. I'm doing a live video
so looks like you're stuck in it forever, not my fault. Good thing you
were wearing hijab," she added as an afterthought as Elizza stared
dumbly at Leedya's phone resting at the base of her mirror for a second before hopping frantically out of the frame. "Umm, where was
I? Oh yeah." Charming smile. "My accessories, the earrings and this
matching necklace if you're not wearing the end of the scarf around
your neck, that would just be overkill. And for makeup I'm wearing..." Elizza gave up. She couldn't find anything underneath the
endless compilation of Leedya's clothing and accessories. She headed
back to her room in defeat.

***

The next morning, as Elizza got ready to leave, she received a
text message from her sister—despite being in the house at the same
time. Sometimes, Leedya just couldn't be bothered to get up.

Leedya: Look at this, lol. Kareema must be bored with her
BFF sick

She attached a screenshot of her phone, which showed that Kareema BenAli took a screenshot of Leedya's latest Snapchat hijab tutorial video.

Leedya: I doubt she took it to get hijab advice on the Gypsy
style LMAO. Maybe she wants me for her brother 😂 😂 😂

Elizza messaged back.

Elizza: Ha. Ha.
Leedya: Jana better watch her back 😂
Elizza: 😶 she probably took a screenshot so she could
show her brother and or friends what a sai3a you are
Leedya: 😂 😂 😂 😂
Leedya: ok I'm done. Things to do and all that. 👋 🤭

"Hey wait," Leedya called as Elizza came into the kitchen to grab breakfast before she left, an amused smile across her face. She was eating breakfast at the kitchen table with Kawthar. "I have to show you something." She pulled out her phone and swiped and scrolled, her fake nails tapping and scratching across the surface (she liked to get fake nails put on but kept them short so it wouldn't interfere with her trade – she was nothing if not professional about it), but frowned in frustration after a few minutes searching. Elizza grew impatient.

"Come on, Leedya, I have to go."

"Sorry but..." swipe scratch swipe tap. "Damn. The post was deleted. So you know how Kareema took that screen shot of my video? Well she took it of you not me, then posted it on her FB wall. And I thought she tagged Tarseen in it, of all people! It had a hashtag of like #Lown3ayoonak or whatever that Nancy Ajram song is. Really freaking weird but as you can see it's been taken down." She mused for a second. "Maybe he wasn't tagged in it I don't know I was just scrolling through a bunch of stuff, but it was just so weird of her to post your picture in the first place. Maybe she meant to send it in a private message." She danced her eyebrows at Elizza.

"Omg that's so shade," Kawthar piped in.

Leedya snorted. "What? You mean shady?"

"Or sketch. I meant sketch. You can't say shade? Shade is to shady as sketch is to sketchy." Leedya laughed even harder.

"Is that not how that works?" Kawthar asked in a small voice.

"Oh my God you're killing me, Kawthar," Leedya said when she could control her laughter. "It's okay just talk normal. You don't have to try to talk cool. You're a doll." For all the world like she was the older one. And in experience and worldliness, perhaps she really was.

Elizza had a weird feeling in the pit of her stomach but shook it off. She didn't have time for this.

"I don't have time for this," she said, and headed upstairs to get her bag and be off.

"Are you sure you don't need me to go with you?" Abu l'Banaat said doubtfully. He had a drawer full of grading to get done, but at a word from his daughter, he would put it aside and accompany her. And make her do half of it on the drive there, of course.

"I'll be fine, Baba."

"*Mish laazim,*" her mother said in annoyance. *This isn't necessary.* "They will bring Jana back when she is better." Elizza just shouldered her bag and hugged her mother goodbye. She eyed her 2003 Honda Accord dubiously. She hoped it would get her there the entire way.

***

It would not be a good thing for Jana to constantly be around people who made her nervous. Elizza thought with worry about how Jana must be feeling. She hated to impose on people. She must be trying to force her immunity to pick up so that she could stop inconveniencing her hosts. Which wouldn't help matters.

Elizza pushed the gas pedal harder. She rarely ever sped, but she couldn't bear the thought of leaving her fragile sister a second longer than she had to by herself. There was something about BenAli's sister—Elizza couldn't put her finger on it. It was something more than the rudeness she'd already displayed. It was more like malevolence, a dislike of seeing others do well. An arrogance, too. Like they were on a different level than the rest of humanity. She wasn't sure it was the best thing for Jana to be made into a pet by such a woman.

By virtue of pressing the gas pedal harder than she usually did, she ran out of gas about twenty minutes away from the hotel. She cursed her luck. She hated pumping gas—especially in these subpar temperatures. In the snow. She got out of the car, willing the gas to pump faster into her car. Why did it seem to be oozing its way out? She jumped up and down to keep herself warm. It didn't help.

Finally her tank was full...enough. She got back into her car and realized she had to pee. So she drove over to the convenience store front and got out of the car, again, to use the bathroom. She finished and got back into her car, the accumulated warmth the heater generated on the drive up almost gone. She switched the ignition on. It tried hard, and did nothing. She tried again. And again. Five times. And then gave up. Her car would not start.

Better call an Uber she couldn't really afford.

***

The hotel room was dark, and had the unpleasant tinge of a vomit odor in the background. It had been unsettlingly easy to get a room key from the reception desk, but it could have been the "all *hijabis* look alike" phenomenon that helped her along.

"Jana?" Elizza said, walking into the room. The temperature was sweltering, and several water bottles were strewn across the floor. Before she could close the door, she heard a rustling behind her. She turned around to find BenAli studying the hotel room number across from theirs. He jumped, startled, and turned around.

"Oh, *salaam*," he said, his handsome face reddening. Elizza stared, waiting for him to continue. He shoved a plastic bag from CVS into her hands, and shoved his hands into the pockets of his coat nervously.

"For your sister," he said, adding, "Sorry, I should have sent Kareema. She…is resting. So, I thought I'd bring it sooner and leave it on your sister's door." With that, he turned around and fled. Elizza went inside and closed the door, inspecting the contents of the bag.

"Oh look," she said, "your suitor brought you…Sprite, saltines, chicken soup, and Pepto-Bismol."

***

Jana was miserable. The worst of her stomach virus hadn't yet come to pass. Elizza hoped she wouldn't catch it from her—one of them needed be able to drive them home. And she still had to make sure they had a competent vehicle to actually get them there. She thought with dread of the car stuck in the convenience store parking lot, slowly getting buried by snow. Well, nothing she could do about it at the moment. There was likely a snow emergency by this point.

Elizza stared out the window. It was a complete white out. They would be stuck there for at least another day—maybe two. She remembered her mother's insistence that she pack an exorbitant amount of clothing for her and Jana and wondered if she'd checked the forecast up here. She wouldn't put it past her.

She opened her computer to check for the Wifi network and connected to the guest portal, but she was denied access unless she paid the exorbitant amount of $10.99 per day, or she could obtain "Free Wifi for the duration of your stay with the purchase of a beverage from our Inn House Café." She sighed. Coffee was probably cheaper than $10.99.

She glanced at Jana, peacefully resting for the moment, then closed her computer, grabbed her folder of business plan materials, threw on an abaya and scarf, and left the room.

***

The café was pretty full. Not to capacity but still more people than you'd expect in an out of the way hotel café. Elizza walked to the counter to wait her turn to pay $4.75 for Wifi access—and her accompanying cup of coffee. Turning to look at the occupants as she stood in line, she spotted Tarseen and BenAli sitting with Kareema at a table. Elizza turned around hastily, trying to hide behind the tall gentleman to her right. She looked back to see Tarseen looking her way, and knew hiding was futile. She took out her phone, trying to look busy and hoping it would keep him from approaching or alerting the others to her presence. She surreptitiously watched the group as she waited to put her order in.

Kareema seemed to be having some sort of argument with BenAli. Tarseen made his way over to where she was standing.

"Kareema is sitting over there," Tarseen said unnecessarily. Elizza turned to look at him, catching Kareema's glare in the background. "What are you having?" he said quickly. "I'm ordering for us." Elizza objected mildly. He insisted gallantly, so she stopped pretending to care (he was rich enough), until he walked away and she remembered why she came there in the first place, muttering, "Wait, my WiFi access…." She shrugged, vowing to buy herself another cup when everyone else left, and walked away to find a seat. She chose her own table, near enough to the group to avoid being rude but hoping to be able to get some work done on her plan.

"Thank you for leaving us the room," Elizza told Kareema, ironically. Jana informed her that Kareema went to stay with her brother in his room when it became clear that Jana was in the throes of some awful stomach bug, leaving Tarseen, who had been sharing a room with BenAli, to book his own room.

Kareema just smiled. "How is Jana doing now?" she asked, when Tarseen returned with everyone's coffee. Her voice sounded awfully solicitous. Tarseen quietly slipped Elizza the receipt, which startled her until she noted that it had a WiFi passcode circled at the bottom. Kareema eyed them both so suspiciously that Elizza almost forgot she'd just been asked a question. Tarseen skirted the table to sit a few chairs away across from BenAli.

"She's doing better, Alhamdulillah." Elizza replied, a few awkward seconds too late.

"Is she still throwing up?" Kareema pressed. Elizza glanced at BenAli. She was not going to discuss her sister's stomach bug symptoms in front of her suitor.

"She's much better," she repeated. "We should be able to leave as soon as this storm passes." She turned pointedly back to her binder, opening her laptop to start doing some research, as overt a sign as any she was capable of that the conversation was over.

"Doing homework, Elizza?" Kareema asked snidely. "Just take a break. Even Tarseen and BenAli don't have their heads buried in work right now, and they run a major business. It's a holiday weekend."

"My MBA requirements won't complete themselves," Elizza replied brightly. She turned back to her work, scrolling through pages of solar panel sale websites to contact suppliers. The others' conversation continued without her. The interactions between the three, however, were so amusing she almost couldn't concentrate on her work.

BenAli and Tarseen had an interesting dynamic. Tarseen was clearly the leader. But BenAli was all lightheartedness and charm. He constantly laughed at his friend and urged him to lighten up. She had never seen Tarseen smile so much—albeit, she hadn't had many interactions with him. They made a good pair—would be the perfect couple, she thought in amusement. Married couples should be paired like that, perfectly balanced opposites.

And Kareema clearly wanted to be one. With Tarseen, that is. He seemed to not know how to treat her, keeping her at somewhat of a distance out of religious decorum but having trouble doing so, with her being the sister of his close friend. They had an informal relationship that was also strained by Tarseen's refusal to wholeheartedly drop his guard. When he laughed at something she said, he paused and *then* laughed, as if weighing the pros and cons of doing so before making a deliberate choice. He was extremely careful with her. Maybe he was afraid of losing his friend? Elizza wondered.

"You need to do something with your money besides just keeping it in cash," Tarseen was telling his friend. "It's doing nothing for you, Ben. Buy some real estate or something."

"That's why I do marketing and you do…everything else. We all gotta stay in our lanes."

"Or hire someone to manage your money for you."

"Kareema manages my money for me," BenAli said.

Tarseen laughed. "Yeah, by spending it." Kareema looked up at Tarseen in mock offense, but clearly enjoying the attention.

"I help him maintain the right image," she said. "Guys need a woman to help them with things like that." She eyed him meaningfully. He caught her gaze and then swiveled his away quickly, landing on Elizza instead. Caught her watching them, and raised an eyebrow at her.

"Working hard, I see," he commented.

"Not very productive, as you can see," she said shortly, standing up to close her laptop and stuff her things into her tote bag. She knocked her business plan binder off of the table in her haste and the contents scattered the floor. He walked over to help her pick it up.

"I wasn't trying to chase you away," he said quietly. Probably to avoid being overheard by his friends. She was bent down trying to pick up some of the papers that landed farther away from the table, but looked up at his comment. Locked eyes with him uncomfortably for a second. He moved his eyes swiftly away and stood up to stare absently at one of the papers in his hand, then absorbing some of the content on the page, exclaimed,

"You're writing your plan to implement in *Libya*?"

"Yes," she said, almost defensively. He said it like she was crazy.

"Why Libya?" he asked.

"That is my ethnicity," was her response. He just waited for a more adequate reply. "I wanted to figure out a way for my entrepreneurship to help others. It's somehow easier to identify needs in Libya than here. Trying to figure out a way to help Libyans inspired a lot of ideas—there's almost limitless potential to help out there."

"We certainly have our work cut out for us," he said. "Whatever it is, it's got to be some ambitious project."

"Libya could use all the people with ambition that will spare them their intellectual creativity."

"Yes," he said, after a pause. An unsatisfying reply, Elizza thought. He just looked at her, his look measuring, assessing, still holding her paper out in front of him. She held out her hand for the paper.

"I have to go check on my sister," she said. He handed her back the paper and turned to rejoin his friends. In the background, Kareema was giving her the stink eye. *Or maybe that's just her resting expression,* Elizza amended mentally. *I'll try to be amicable, for Jana's sake.*

***

Elizza woke up the next morning feeling hopeful. She felt Jana's head—no fever. And she hadn't thrown up in over 12 hours. Progress. They should be able to go home soon. She looked out the window. No more snow, and the roads looked like they were mostly clear. She should be able to get her car sorted. If she got moving quickly, maybe they could even check out of the hotel on time. But first—breakfast.

She walked warily into the breakfast area, looking around for the other guests they knew. A few other Muslim families, probably stuck at the hotel because of the storm, in town for the same wedding Jana attended. But she thought she was free of the others, until she saw Tarseen sitting by himself, laptop open, at a table in a far corner of the room. Looking bright-faced and ready for the morning ahead in a tan sweater and dark-wash jeans, making Elizza feel a little drab in her long open-front sweater she threw over a t-shirt and old pair of jeans. He looked up and saw her, hesitating a second before tossing her one flick of his wrist that was supposed to be a wave. She nodded her head in response, got her food, and tried to find the farthest empty table from him at which to sit. She found one about four tables away—it would do.

She munched on her muffin and eggs and took out her phone to Google the convenience store where her car was parked. She then called the number.

"Hey, whatchya need?" a deep voice asked through the phone. Elizza was momentarily taken aback. Did she have the wrong number?

"Umm, hi. Is this the Speedway off of exit 40?" The background noise was hard to identify.

"Last time I checked," the man replied, his tone sounding bored. "Hold up—no wait, that one doesn't work. You're gunna have to park at another one." She heard some shuffling, then, "Sorry. Go ahead."

"Okay. I'm calling about my car," she went on, describing its make and model. "I just wanted to assure you guys I am going to move it this morning."

"Oh that one? Yeah we wondered about that. We just had it towed."

"Towed?" *Damn.* "But … I couldn't even get it yesterday! It was a snow emergency."

"Yeah, we waited until this morning, but since we didn't hear from anyone, we had to get it moved." She wanted to cry. But the person at the other end of the line was giving her the tow yard information and she needed to be writing it down.

"Hold on a second," she said as she searched frantically for a pen and paper, looking around the room. To her chagrin, Tarseen was in rapt attention to her telephone conversation. After staring uselessly at her for a second, he pulled a pen out of his pocket and waved it at her. She ran over to him and wrote down the tow information on her hand, hanging up her phone afterward.

"Thanks," she said shortly, before placing it back on the table and turning to walk away.

"Wait," he said. She turned to face him. "Give me your keys. I'll go get the car."

"What? No, it's fine. I got it."

"Obviously something is wrong with it if you left it at a gas station."

"I can deal with it. I have roadside assistance," she added, desperately hopeful they could actually help her.

"What are you going to do if you can't fix it? Leave it there and stay here another day? Just give me the keys. I'll go take a look at it." She looked down at the keys in her hand, wanting so badly to hand the problem off to someone else, but pride getting in the way. Then she thought of how long she'd have to leave Jana alone to go deal with the car issue, and for her sake, grudgingly handed over her keys and turned wordlessly around to go pack her bags—they would leave whether her car was ready or not, she vowed. But she felt something nudge her hand slightly and jumped.

"Sorry," Tarseen said, almost blushing. "I need to see the tow yard location." She held out her hand as he added the location to his Google Maps, trying not to cringe with awkwardness, then fled to her room.

***

"Your car battery just had some corrosion," Tarseen said an hour later. Elizza was sitting at the café, finding Jana still sleeping in the room and unwilling to disturb her, and somewhat anxious about her car. She hated handing over the responsibility of it to another person, but he had insisted. And anyway, he was a guy. Didn't it do something for their egos to help damsels in distress with things they thought they had a monopoly on knowing about? Like car maintenance? Fixing things? Cooking outdoors?

She looked up at Tarseen. He had his hand outstretched, holding the keys out in front of her. She took them silently.

"A lot of it," he added. She lifted a brow at him. How gallant of him to point that out. "Anyway, I took it to AutoPlace to get a new one. It looked like it hadn't been replaced in years."

"Well, thank you," she responded, but almost winced at the ungrateful sound of her voice. He did just do something nice for her.

"You should take better care of your car," was his response. "If you insist on driving it long distances." With that, he walked away, and any gratitude she had left evaporated like a droplet of water on a sweltering afternoon.

Elizza went up to their room to wake her sister. Jana was really feeling a lot better. Elizza was happy she did not have to worry her about the car, at least. But she was otherwise conflicted about the situation. She was bothered by the fact that Tarseen would assume things about her character based on her car maintenance habits. And then she was bothered even more by the fact that she was bothered.

Why should she even care? She shook her head, forcing her mind in a different direction. She hated to dwell on the uncomfortable.

She packed both of their bags swiftly, threw away all evidence of her sister's illness, after which she thoroughly washed her hands, and efficiently packed it all onto a bell cart and filed it all and her sister, still somewhat weak, into the hotel elevator. Twenty minutes to checkout before being charged for an additional day—they emphatically refused to offer a later checkout time.

The elevator opened to the hotel lobby, revealing BenAli and his friend checking out, Kareema lounging on a couch, waiting for them to finish. Elizza sent Jana to sit by her friend, and stood behind the men to check out, noticing in annoyance Kareema scoot over infinitesimally, as if she was afraid proximity to Jana would make her sick.

The men finished and turned to find Elizza behind them.

"I hope your sister is feeling better," BenAli said politely. "Did she get..." he started to ask, then stopped in embarrassment, glancing for a second at his friend. Elizza got the hint.

"Jana was fully supplied with everything she needed to get better," she replied. He nodded his head and walked over to talk to Jana—and she saw him get the keys from Jana to take their bags to their car. Elizza eyed his friend warily, until she remembered she had completely forgotten to ask him how much the tow fee was. She rectified that now.

"I'm sorry, I completely forgot earlier. Let me—" she stopped to pull out her wallet, hoping desperately she had enough cash. Or at least a check.

"I'm not taking anything," he said. She looked at him in exasperation.

"I can't let you pay my tow fee. And for the new battery. It was like, what, two hundred dollars?"

"It wasn't that much," he said, smiling. "Really, it's fine." She ignored him, opening her wallet to pull out four twenty-dollar bills—it was all she had.

"This is all my cash, but—"

"I need the good deeds," he insisted, cutting her off. She was going to argue with him, but he stopped her. "Why don't you do this? Donate it somewhere on my behalf. If you feel like it's necessary. But

I don't want it back." He turned to walk away, and then halted to say, "hey, we'll stay until you leave, just to make sure your car is okay. Oh, and I'm sorry if I implied you didn't take good care of your car. I'm… sure you did your best." Then he walked out of the building. Elizza huffed. If anything, his apology was more infuriating than his original comment.

Chapter Seven

Kamaal BenTaleb posted.

My ears heard and my eyes saw the Prophet (PBUH) when he spoke, "Anybody who believes in Allah and the Last Day, should serve his neighbor generously, and anybody who believes in Allah and the Last Day should serve his guest generously by giving him his reward." It was asked, "What is his reward, O Allah's Messenger?" He (PBUH) said, "(To be entertained generously) **for a day and a night with high quality of food and the guest has the right to be entertained for three days** (with ordinary food) and if he stays longer, what he will be provided with will be regarded as *Sadaqa* (a charitable gift). And anybody who believes in Allah and the Last Day should talk what is good or keep quiet (i.e., abstain from all kinds of dirty and evil talks)." (Sahih al-Bukhari)

Kamaal BenTaleb tagged Abu l'Banaat in a post.

~

The long, what was supposed to be restful, holiday weekend— wasn't. Elizza was looking forward to getting home, even though she knew she would be back to her busy school schedule tomorrow, hoping that maybe she could recoup the next weekend. But her hopes were shattered when she overheard the following conversation:

"*Hayati*, we're going to have an overnight guest this weekend, so get the *manadeer* from whoever borrowed them last," Abu l'Banaat informed his wife.

"A guest? What guest?" Umm ul'Banaat was all curiosity.

"The *manadeer, habibti.*"

"Fathiyah borrowed them. Who is it?"

"She has had them for what, two years now? Well, tell her that unfortunately our hiatus on having guests has come to an end and we need them back."

"What guest? I need to know so I know what to cook."

"Better you call than me. Would the menu change based on the person?"

"Is it a married person?"

"No."

"Young?"

"Yes."

"Libyan?"

"Yes." Their mother's excitement grew with each answer.

"Then yes, of course it would change." She built up such an ideal in her mind of this potential guest that when he finally revealed it was his cousin coming for a visit, her excitement was dampened considerably.

This particular cousin was an anomaly, being the son of an uncle of her husband's that formerly cheated him out of some land that he was supposed to inherit when his father passed away in Libya. There was an unwritten understanding of how their father's property would be distributed between the two brothers after his death, but when the sad event actually came to pass, his older brother conveniently forgot their oral agreement, instead dividing up the land as an even 50/50 of their father's consolidated 12 hectares of land, but reserving for himself the most valuable pieces. What did his nephew, who was living the good life in America, need with land in Libya anyway? he argued. He was lucky to be given anything. Abu l'Banaat did not possess the type of personality that would contest such an issue, too ashamed to fight with his own family about a purely financial issue.

When his son needed a letter of invitation for his son to get a visitor visa to the United States, however, he did not hesitate to ask his nephew to fill out the papers, and did not take it kindly when Abu l'Banaat refused. Consequently, he did not have much to do with his cousin, who was several years younger than he and was doing the bulk of his growing up in Libya at the time that Abu l'Banaat had already immigrated to the United States. He was surprised to be contacted by Kamaal after so many years, asking to stay with him for a few days as he attended an Imam training being held at their local masjid. He was inclined to be on good terms with his cousin, not feeling it was fair to hold the sins of the father against the son. So he graciously accepted to host his cousin, thinking also with amusement of how excited his wife would be to host a single bachelor in her household. He presumed she would forget the antipathy she felt for his family members (she had a lot of plans for the money they would have gotten selling such valuable pieces of land in Libya) for the sake of her marital schemes.

Yes, Umm ul'Banaat was disappointed that her husband was teasing her, making their guest sound grander than he turned out to be. But she rallied admirably. It wasn't everyday you had an eligible bachelor staying in your house, and it was not every mother who had five girls in need of one. She called her girls downstairs to help. She had a plan to marshal.

***

"Fathiyah," Umm ul'Banaat said into the phone. They had already exchanged their mandatory two minutes of "how are you?", "how is your health?", "how is your family?", "how is your family's health?" and news updates. Now it was time to get to business. "We are so excited to have a guest. But we do not have a separate bed, so—" Fortunately, Fathiyah took the hint, and just barely remembered that she was in possession of her friend's *manadeer*—but unfortunately getting the number in her possession wrong.

"*Saamhini*, Fathiyah," Umm ul'Banaat interrupted. *Forgive me, Fathiyah.* "It was so long ago, but didn't you borrow three of them?" More talking into the phone. Umm ul'Banaat's face fell; she couldn't press the point now. "You must be right. What is a good time for Abu l'Banaat to pick them up?" At this point, she was expecting Fathiyah to offer to have her husband bring them. But alas, Fathiyah responded with a window of time that might be appropriate. "*Jazak Allah khair*," *May Allah reward you*, she said, before hanging up, and sitting down to rest on her couch for a few moments and lamenting that she didn't have more considerate friends.

***

The doorbell rang, announcing the arrival of their visitor. Umm ul'Banaat looked over her five daughters, trying to decide whom to send to answer the door. Not Jana, she was almost taken. Leedya? No, she'd say something offensive. Kawthar had no grace yet, and Maryam would just refuse. She sighed, getting ready to order her second-oldest daughter to answer the door, when Abu l'Banaat disobligingly opened it himself. She would have to make these decisions more quickly.

Their visitor walked in, and was ushered into the second living room area that they used when they had male guests visiting Abu l'Banaat, cheating them all out of a look at their visitor. Again, her husband upended her plans. She needed to have a talk with him—they would never accomplish anything if she didn't enlist his help.

Umm ul'Banaat stood thinking for a quick second. She wanted Kamaal to see her daughters, but wanted to preserve the idea that they were distantly related enough to marry. It was easier to get your daughters married within the family in Libya—she never wore hijab in front of any of her male cousins. Abu l'Banaat wouldn't hear of allowing his daughters to do that, however, saying the cultural practice wasn't consistent with Islam. He could be strict about some things.

"Well, go sit down," she ordered her girls when they just stood confusedly in the hall.

"A beautiful home," Kamaal was telling his cousin. "Very nicely decorated." At his cousin's silence, he paused, and offered a change of subject.

"I was embarrassed to hear about the feud between you and my father, and sorry to hear others in the family say that he was not fair in the way he divided the land." Elizza, hearing the remark as they made their way down the hall, shook her head in amusement. Apologies are cheaper than offering to have new surveys drawn.

The girls filed through the living room door then, and he stopped to look up, only to lower his gaze awkwardly when they passed, for all the world as if they strode into the room naked. Kamaal was a heavier man, with unexceptional brown eyes in a round face, and hair cut very short. His expression was solemn and sincere. Abu l'Banaat surveyed his girls critically, and slapped his cousin on the shoulder in amusement.

"If you look at the floor the whole time," he told Kamaal, "talking will be very difficult. No need to be shy, Kamaal. We are all family in this room. But if my daughters sitting in here makes you uncomfortable—"

"Not at all," he said, embarrassed. He looked up to offer them a shy "*assalaamu'alaikum*," and was about to look back at the floor subconsciously when Elizza caught his eye. He made a conscious effort not to look away, and in doing so, left his gaze on her for far too long. Now she was the uncomfortable one. Leedya saw the exchange and almost audibly snorted, waiting until Elizza looked her way before holding onto her ring finger and winking, getting a glare in return. But Umm ul'Banaat had other thoughts, catching the exchange of looks. From what she could tell, their guest liked what he saw. If one of her daughters didn't have a marriage proposal by the end of his visit, she thought, she would eat a spoonful of the spiciest *hareesa*.

✳ ✳ ✳

The next few days in the house were awkward for the girls. It was difficult to know what to do in the house with a male guest lingering about. They had to try to avoid being alone with him in any room, for the sake of Islamic etiquette, and he seemed to pop up in all of their usual haunts. He made himself at home, as Abu l'Banaat advised him he should. He stayed watching Arabic television in their family room, quickly switching the channel from whatever Syrian drama he was watching to a channel giving religious lectures when he heard anyone getting ready to enter the room. At midday, her father's office was off limits because he would be in it, resting on the *mindaar* he was given to place on the floor in lieu of a guest bed, taking his afternoon *gayla*. Several times a day he was seen rummaging through their refrigerator between meals. The girls were somewhat put off to find their favorite snacks missing out of the fridge or pantry, Kamaal having devoured the last of them. Leedya was ready to commit murder when her breakfast protein shake went missing. The "imam training" he came to complete at their local masjid seemed to take up very little of his time.

"*Usburoo, maalishi, ya banaat, tawa shwaya wa birowhu,*" their mother scolded. *Be patient, girls. Just a little longer and he will be leaving, anyway.* "Go buy your sister some more, Elizza." Elizza really didn't have time. She had miles of work to get done, still a packet of stuff to do to graduate. But then she thought of the relief she would feel to get out of the house for a bit, and put on her jacket to go to the store.

She bumped into Kamaal on her way out the door. He looked at her for a long second, and then looked at the floor. Elizza could respect a man who consciously made an effort to lower his gaze—as long as he was consistent about it. He alternated staring at her and awkwardly avoiding her gaze, seeming to be confused himself about whether it was okay to look at her or not. He seemed to bump into her quite often around the house, disturbingly. She said nothing, only moved to the side to go around him, as he seemed to be frozen in place before her. Her keys jiggled as she grabbed them hastily out of her purse.

"You're leaving, sister?" he queried, turning to face her. She opened the door before answering, sending a quick, "have to run to the store," over her shoulder, trying to escape.

"*Stanni shwaya,*" he told her. *Wait a second.* "Maybe I can get what you need from the store."

"It's…" she wavered, thinking quickly. "It's a personal item." He blushed, but was undeterred.

"I can't let you go by yourself. Let me get in my car and follow behind you, to make sure you get there safely. You shouldn't have to go to the store alone at night." Elizza exhaled, exasperated.

"Really, there's no need," she said, at a loss about what she could say. She would just go tomorrow if this man was going to try to force her to let him follow her. She stepped fully inside the door, ready to take her coat off and flee to her room, when her father stepped outside of his office.

"Oh, don't worry about that," Abu l'Banaat said. "I'll go with Elizza. But we appreciate your kind offer," he said comfortingly.

"No problem at all. It would have been no trouble." Abu l'Banaat just smiled and opened the hall closet to get his coat before ushering Elizza out the door and into their car sitting in the driveway. Elizza huffed angrily, climbing into the passenger side and slamming the door behind her. Her father turned on the car, then glanced over to get a good look at her face, before bursting into laughter.

***

The indignities of having Kamaal for a houseguest did not end there. The first morning after his first night as their guest, their mother decided to institute a new family practice. The second the pre-dawn fajr prayer dawned, she knocked on both girls' rooms to wake them all. Elizza looked drowsily at the time on her phone and groaned. *I had twenty minutes left of sleep before my fajr alarm would be going off,* she thought. Umm ul'Banaat popped her head into their room.

"Wake up," she told them unceremoniously. "Do *wudhu* and come downstairs to pray *fajr* with your father." And Kamaal, she didn't say.

"Mama," Elizza protested.

"*Uskuti,*" her mother said. *Be quiet.* "We have a *hafidh* and a real imam in the house. We should take advantage of our luck. And Elizza, don't you dare wear that terrible prayer outfit you wear to pray in everyday," she added, before leaving the room. Elizza was just reaching for it. *Bizarre,* she thought. And then her heart sank. *Oh no. Oh no no no.* She should have suspected—but then, her mother seemed to have given up on marrying her off lately, so she had let her guard down. But there was no denying after that statement—she was offering Elizza up on a platter for their houseguest. Elizza glanced at her prayer outfit and screwed up her face in determination. *Just let her try.*

By sheer will, and to the other girls' surprise, Umm ul'Banaat crushed Leedya's complaints and refused to give in to her pleas to be left alone.

"I can't pray," Leedya lied.

"You just had your period a week ago," their mother responded, and pulled the blankets off of Leedya's bed, letting them fall to the floor. Kawthar drowsily made her way to the bathroom all five girls had to share, and collapsed in a seated position against the wall all the way down to the floor when she saw it was occupied. By

Maryam, who uncomplainingly got out of bed to go do wudhu first. She always woke up right at the dawn of *fajr*.

Umm ul'Banaat glared at Elizza when she saw what she was wearing upon entering the living room for prayer. When she got home from university later that afternoon, her prayer outfit was nowhere to be found.

Their mother repeated the practice every morning of the remainder of Kamaal's stay. It would be an admirable thing to do as a family, Elizza mused, if they actually did it on a regular basis and not just for show in front of their guest. Kamaal was always invited, and always accepted, to lead the morning prayer and any other prayer they held together. Leedya was always irritable and moody when woken up so early. If any of her sisters put their foot anywhere near hers she stomped on it ruthlessly just to exhibit her annoyance with the situation. On normal days, she liked to set her alarm for ten minutes before dawn. Maryam would pray serenely and calmly with everyone, remarking that first *fajr* after being forced to pray with their guest, "We should do this every morning."

"Then Leedya would be perpetually 'not praying,'" Elizza laughed, her amusement lighting up her face. And then Kamaal came into the room, stopping to gaze at Elizza for a second before taking his place as Imam, wiping Elizza's smile away.

Chapter Eight

Umm ul'Banaat added LazyLizza to a group. Local Weddings on a Budget

Elizza had two things bothering her that kept her from falling asleep again after *fajr*—before she had to wake up to go to the university. One was that look from Kamaal, a sort of piercing, assessing and unshy gaze that seemed to have graduated from the embarrassed glance he shot at her when encountering her unexpectedly in the hallways of their house or alone in the kitchen. It was a gaze with an intention behind it. He almost didn't seem to care if her father noticed. She thought about what she could do to discourage his interest. She had already made sure to wear the most dingy hijabs and abayas she could find in her closet whenever she was around him. Unfortunately, her most horrendous and old clothing kept disappearing out of her closet. She tried to voice the most outrageous of her beliefs, opinions, and plans for her personal future in his presence, just to put him off. Like,

"People should wait until their mid-thirties to have children. It's hard on women when they have children early. They end up having to put their entire lives on hold." Their mother was making an early breakfast (another new "tradition" begun in the house for the benefit of their guest—but one that Elizza secretly hoped would continue after he left), and Kamaal just popped his head in to see if he could grab a plate of food and take it back to his room, deeming it improper to eat with the girls at the table crammed in the corner of their kitchen for the eating of informal family meals, since Abu l'Banaat couldn't be bothered to wake up that early to eat breakfast—he always insisted his lectures be scheduled after 10 a.m. Kamaal looked a little crestfallen that the food wasn't yet ready.

"That age can't be very far off for you," he responded, smiling, before looking at the state of the eggs cooking on the kitchen stove and determining to come back again in exactly seven minutes. He popped back out again, and Leedya burst into merry laughter. "I'm starting to enjoy him being here," she said. Elizza got up to leave; her stomach rumbled, but she told it to shut up and promised it that she would grab some coffee on her way to the university, slipping out of the kitchen so quietly her mother didn't notice and she avoided her mother's questions about why she had to leave so early.

The next occasion she found to attempt to offend him was when she saw him talking to her father and Tarseen at *jumaa* prayer that Friday. Maryam and Elizza were on their way to pick up Jana from her job at the daycare so they could all go to *jumaa*, as was their practice most Fridays. They tried to rope Leedya and Kawthar into going as well, but those two were usually busy doing other things, not bothering to ask to be scheduled to work, or scheduling their own college classes, so they could attend the masjid congregation. Elizza almost thought she would have to come up with an excuse to avoid going as a thought materialized in her mind—*what if Kamaal is giving the khutbah today?* She didn't think she wanted to listen to any khutbah he was responsible for writing. She liked to go to *jumaa* every Friday for that faith boost she got listening to the thoughtful and concise sermon given by various community leaders, and sometimes special visitors, at their local masjid. Their local masjid had a good track record of choosing superb orators. But she made Maryam look up who the speaker would be that day just to make sure—without revealing her true aim in asking the question. What she told Maryam was,

"Hey, make sure the 1:15 prayer is being given by a native English speaker," because she knew that Maryam would object to going to the one in Arabic, as their understanding of the lecture would suffer somewhat if he spoke a dialect other than Libyan Arabic, and she always worried that their *jumaa* prayer wouldn't count unless they comprehended what was said 100%. Maryam unlocked her phone and pulled up the masjid website.

"Hmm. Oh, interesting. Yeah, it's English, Elizza." Maryam said. Elizza turned her head around to stare at Maryam in the backseat.

"Well, who is it?" she demanded.

"Elizza! You're driving! Look at the road." She obliged, but found Maryam's face in the rearview mirror and continued to glare.

"Firas Tarseen is giving the khutbah today," she said, after her heart stopped beating so fast. She had been in a mild car accident when Leedya was driving, a result of Leedya's intextication, and was probably suffering post-traumatic stress syndrome as a result of that event. It made her a really infuriating back seat driver.

"Really?" Elizza said aloud. "What makes him qualified?" Her voice oozed skepticism. Some people really liked to put themselves forward no matter what the occasion.

"Umm, I'm pretty sure he's a *hafidh*," Maryam replied.

"So? That doesn't necessarily qualify—" Elizza interrupted, hot on her topic.

Maryam interrupted her back, "—and it says here he studied *fiqh* for a year at the Islamic university of—"

"Okay, I get it," Elizza said, irritated. "Never mind."

Maryam smiled, her face lighting up the rearview mirror. Elizza smiled involuntarily in return. It was nice to see Maryam smile. She had an understated beauty that was never fully realized because she did not grace the world with her smile very often. No matter how many times her sisters teased her that she should do it more often because a smile is *sadaqa*.

"What are you smiling about?" she finally asked.

"You hate so much when you're wrong. Why do you get so surly when that Tarseen guy is mentioned? It's so weird. You're normally almost never in a bad mood."

Elizza stayed silent.

***

The *khutbah* was surprisingly good. Who knew Tarseen could speak eloquently on topics that didn't have to do with international business, Elizza mused. His Qur'anic references were all on point, discussing the hope that the Qur'an gives to even the most ardent of sinners that they could be forgiven.

The girls waited outside of the masjid to say hello to their father before leaving—another Friday tradition. To Elizza's chagrin, Abu l'Banaat came out side by side, and in deep conversation, with BenAli, Tarseen and Kamaal. She was on the verge of telling her sisters she forgot something she had to do so they could leave right away, but their father spotted them and began directing the group in their general direction, then left the other three trailing slightly behind to hug his daughters and ask how their days went. BenAli strode over to stand next to her father, and to try not to look at Jana, and tapped his shoulder to get his attention.

"Don't forget, not this Saturday but next Saturday me and Tarseen were roped in to buying a whole lamb for everyone to share; someone joked that our business needed *barakah*. I just want to make sure you are there, too." Elizza smiled to herself, but kept an ear open to another interesting conversation going on between Tarseen and Kamaal. She didn't know which one she wanted to listen to more.

"...in your khutbah where you said the companions lived in a time of prostitution and other prevalent evils. We shouldn't point that out to the ummah. It's wrong." Kamaal, was saying to Tarseen.

"But true," Tarseen replied. "Are Muslims supposed to cover up every negative blip along the way to enhance our own image?"

"I will be there. My wife will offer to make something, so let me know what you need," her father replied. BenAli looked awkward.

"Just men," he said quickly, shooting her sisters an apologetic glance. "Tarseen wanted..." he trailed off.

"No, but we shouldn't give young people license to sin by making them think sinning is just emulating the *sahaba* before they were given Islam," Kamaal insisted. Now she was transfixed on this conversation—she sort of loved arguments. The rawness of people's personalities always revealed itself with aplomb.

"Young people need to know that anyone can reform their ways. And besides, you don't know anything about being a young person who grew up here. So maybe you're not really competent to judge."

"I'm an *imam*..." he said, his voice dripping indignation. But he spotted Elizza and seemed to forget that he was in the middle of a conversation.

"*Assalaamu alaikum*," he said, seemingly to all of the sisters, but angling his body slightly Elizza's way and allowing his gaze to zero in on her. Tarseen noticed. Elizza noticed Tarseen notice and blushed. *This had to stop,* Elizza thought, determined. So she turned to Tarseen.

"Great *khutbah*," she said, her voice a touch overly enthusiastic. He smiled slightly in return, but his face looked more confused than pleased by the compliment. "I have to say that I don't agree with the idea of being overly harsh on people who sin. Sometimes the only window of opportunity you have with them is giving them hope in the mercy of Allah, because it's too easy for them to forget that and think they might as well pile on more sins since they're doomed anyway."

"Yes," Tarseen replied quietly. "That was what I was getting at."

"But sometimes focusing too much on Allah's mercy seems to discount the work of those who have spent their entire lives trying to please Allah," Kamaal responded, his voice a little heated. He turned fully toward Elizza, seeming to block Tarseen out of the conversation. "It makes it seem too easy, and like it is pointless to work hard." Elizza was almost happy. Kamaal was really and truly riled now. Now what could she say to put off his interest once and for all?

"But every single person could use a reminder," she replied. "No one is perfect. We've *all* sinned at one point or another. Every. Single. One of us."

"In different degrees," Tarseen said, smilingly. And diffusing the implied insult of her statement. She glanced his way shortly before turning to Kamaal again.

"Sure. I heard a funny quote once that is relevant here. By a homosexual writer from the 1900s. 'Every saint has a past and every sinner has a future.'" Kamaal's face flushed at the word "homosexual," Tarseen just stared at her sardonically, and Elizza turned triumphantly around to stand next to her father, who had been listening to the entire exchange, his hands comfortably ensconced in his coat pockets, and taking in all.

***

Despite Elizza's attempts to put off Kamaal, however, he still seemed unwaveringly interested for some weird reason she could not fathom. And she was worried it would give her ulcers.

The other thing that was keeping her awake was a meeting she had that morning, scheduled at her advisor's insistence that she meet with Firas Tarseen, to get his input on her business plan.

"I sent him a copy of your business plan," her advisor said, maddeningly. *Why?* she wanted to scream. "I brought up your name when I passed him in the hall and mentioned your project. He said you should meet with him. So I made you an appointment Monday at 10 am." She tried to smile in return and mumbled a, "thank you," before she walked out of his office.

She gave up trying to get some sleep, and flipped on her phone light so she could look through her closet without turning on the light and waking Jana. Not that she'd mind or object, the dear, dear girl. But Elizza always hated being woken up early by their bright bedroom light, so she would be considerate of her sister. Now what sort of outfit said "bite me" the clearest? Her phone light lit across her black, power blazer her penny-pinching self had uncharacteristically shelled out over $100 for, hoping the price tag would give her the extra confidence she would need to land a stellar job. *That's the one.* Now she just needed to find the perfect hijab.

***

The silence was deafening. Tarseen and Elizza sat on opposite sides of a long, beat-up wooden office desk in a tiny courtesy office given to him by the university for use during his visit, in the damp and semi-isolated basement office space of the business college building, housed down the hall from the room full of cubicles they allotted to business students given teaching scholarships and in need of a place to hold office hours. Elizza always felt bad for them (and grateful for the Business Women's Association scholarship she was awarded that kept her from having to accept a teaching appointment to pay her tuition and making up one of their number) as they shunted their ways like goblins to the very bottom of the building, so low even the elevator wasn't built to go down there. Elizza's advisor sat next to Elizza in a chair placed more at the corner of the desk. Tarseen *seemed* to be reviewing notes about her plan, looking up at her occasionally to find her staring him down, before returning his eyes immediately back to the papers on his desk. But the notes were printed on two 8" x 11.5" pages, spread out side by side before him. And they were double-spaced. They clearly didn't take that long to review.

He had taken one look at her in her when she came to his office, her advisor trailing behind, looking askance at her black power blazer and the hundred-dollar bill print scarf she decided was a perfectly ironic match (Leedya gave it to her as a present, thinking it was an appropriate accessory for a business major to own—which she got for free from one of her clothing sponsors) and letting his gaze slide away. After that, it never seemed to make its way back. She cleared her throat in annoyance. And then he punished her by uttering a sentence that pulled all of her vulnerabilities out from the depths of her soul where she hid them.

"So, it's a cute little idea, but how you're going to implement this is not at all clear."

Elizza bristled at the word "cute." She knew that she had some major work to do before she could even begin its practical implementation. She worried that her business plan was sounding too much like science fiction. She had a grand vision for what Libya could look like if only everyone could work together, and what measures could be taken to solve common problems. Limited energy access. The poisoning of local water sources due to carelessness and the lack of regulation—which was due to the lack of governance. She wanted to build a business that would allow residential access to clean energy and water generation. She also wanted to help the country conserve its oil wealth by giving people incentives to switch to solar and wind power—and switch municipal energy sources completely to those things. She had done her research thoroughly, contacted clean energy suppliers, and thought of ways to initially fund it. Found prices that would enable the company to sell at a price affordable for the average homeowner in Libya. She was just hung up on the security of the business—how to navigate the special interest mafias that might stand in the way. She didn't need someone to point all of this out to her, however. She knew it already. And hearing someone criticize the thing about herself that she considered defined her really hit home.

Elizza's entrepreneurial spirit was born out of her family circumstances. She knew that she was privileged to be brought up in a middle class family in the United States, when the alternative was to be stuck in a country currently suffering the well-intentioned but devastating combustion of a revolution. But she did feel the effects of her upbringing, one of five daughters to a man bringing in scarcely more than $50,000 per year. She felt the trappings of a middle class lifestyle, sort of being stuck in a hamster's wheel, unable to break out of it, always powering someone else's dream.

But business was different. You were the master of your own destiny. You owned your hard work. You benefited and suffered from your own choices. You could bury yourself in an early grave of lifelong debt, or you could soar to unimaginable heights and actually change the world. The possibilities were endless. You were only limited by the ceiling of your own capability. And sometimes, by the doubts of others that wiggled their way into your brain and killed your momentum, and even your conviction, if you allowed them to affect you.

"What's your plan for getting people to take you seriously as a business woman in Libya? And what solid connections have you made in the business world there?" he pressed, when she just sat there looking at him dumbly.

"Excuse me? As a woman?"

"That is what I asked, yes." He exchanged a small smile with her advisor.

"What does being a woman have anything to do with it? I have a Libyan born father and he taught me that women are just as capable as men of doing anything."

"I didn't say anything about capability. Just that you have a more difficult road ahead of you, as a woman."

"I think I can manage, thanks, *despite* being a female."

"Right, so that's why I am asking you…. What are your solid, real world plans for breaking into the Libyan business world?"

"I'll do the same things that other businesses do—network, advertise, audience targeting—"

"But how are you going to make them take notice of *you* as a female business owner and not dismiss you?"

"Maybe they will do me the dignity of seeing the value of my ideas and not pre-judging my products or services based on my gender."

"But you don't have a solid idea yet, that's my point. And honestly, you're a fool if you think your gender will have nothing to do with how your business is perceived. You at least have to concede me that."

"I have tons of ideas."

"You have an idealistic plan to 'help' Libya with your business, with no practical considerations whatsoever. As an investor, I wouldn't invest a dollar in your business as it is now. I'd have to be very concerned about whether I'd ever get my money back. One militia could just waltz over and take over your windmill solar panel store or factory, you never made clear whether you were retail or wholesale, and all your money goes out the window."

"Okay Kevin O'Leary." He laughed. "Well obviously I'm still formulating it. That's why it's called a plan, and I'm still a student."

"But it should be one of your first considerations when planning the business. As a woman with few or no resources in the business world in Libya, no knowledge of how it exists within the socio-political order, and the daughter of an expat with no resources, how do you think you are going to get people to take you seriously?" Her advisor looked at her expectantly, waiting for her answer. She sat mutely.

"I have an uncle who lives in Libya," she said finally. "He's offered to help…. I'm supposed to go there this summer."

"Well," her advisor said abruptly, breaking in. He sounded slightly bored. "I think you two can carry on the rest of this conversation without me." He stood up, getting ready to pat Elizza on the back, but glanced at Tarseen's hard face and placed his hands in his pockets before opening the office door to walk out. "You should listen to him Elizza—they're very helpful questions he's asking," he said over his shoulder before walking out and closing the door behind him.

"So what's your problem?" she said as soon as her advisor vacated the room. "You don't think a woman can or should try to change things for the better? Women shouldn't have ambitions to change the world?"

"Maybe you shouldn't put words in my mouth," he said quietly.

"So?" she almost shrieked at him. Getting words out of this man was impossible.

He exhaled his breath sharply. "Honestly, I think it is an amazing vision. You've got a lot of really creative and innovative ideas. Any country that had an energy system like this implemented would go on to do ever greater things." Pause. "But it is not simple to apply this in Libya by any means. If you want to B.S. your way through your plan and write anything, I can give you enough answers to keep your professors happy. But the truth is, it is really impractical for Libya right now in its current political climate. It would be almost impossible to accomplish. Alone." His answer left her deflated, with her anger oddly defused as well. Maybe it wouldn't hurt to take her advisor's advice.

"The way I see it, Libya has the opposite problem as before," she finally answered. "Before it was a problem with restrictive regulation. Now, there's pretty much anarchy, the problem of too much freedom for everyone, a sort of Hobbesian conundrum where things become even more restrictive because of the chaos."

"Yes," he answered shortly. Oh, for God's sake.

"Well, how have you been successful?" she asked again. "Or maybe you don't want to share that information with a potential competitor?" He shot her an amused smile.

"What specifically do you want to know?"

"There's inequality in the way that resources are distributed between cities," Elizza remarked. "What needs to happen to ensure more even distribution of energy resources?"

"Too much," he replied shortly. "It's not really feasible at this point in Libya."

"How so? Anything is possible if you have the resources to accomplish it—or if the people have the will."

"This is a project for a more stable, probably utopian society that doesn't exist anywhere in the world, let alone in the Arab world." Elizza sat up straighter in her chair.

"Give me the laundry list," she countered.

"An actual internationally recognized—let alone nationally recognized—undisputed central government."

"Okay."

"Neutralization of militias."

"Okay."

"Containment of corruption and resource theft."

"Okay," she said again, making notes. She refused to be put off.

"Stopping other countries from interfering in Libya's politics or starting proxy wars. You think you can manage all of that?"

"I already thought about all of the obstacles that stand in my way—I am trying to figure out a solution. You're a successful businessman who does business in Libya. How do you deal with all of this stuff?"

"I certainly have a less idealistic vision; I prefer to deal in practicalities. People would have done what you're trying to do already if it was possible."

"So what's your 'practical' advice?"

"The most valuable advice I can give to a new business in Libya is that you can't seem to be innovating, even if that is what you're doing. Nothing makes people more nervous in times of instability when it comes to spending their money than being the first person to try out something new."

"Like being a solo female business owner in Libya? Because, as you know, there's not much I can do about that fact." He looked her in the eyes then, turning the full power of his gaze upon her in a way that he refused to do before. She was trapped by his eyes like a deer in headlights, couldn't look away herself. He was the first to glance away, saying finally,

"You're a smart woman. I'm sure you will figure that part out."

Chapter Nine

Umm ul'Banaat liked an article, This week's edition of "Five Things You Didn't Know You Should Be Worried About."

Umm ul'Banaat tagged Maryam B, LeedyaMinLeebya, ThatRiverInHeaven, LazyLizza, and Jana bint Leebee in an article, This week's edition of "Five Things You Didn't Know You Should Be Worried About."

LazyLizza posted on Umm ul'Banaat's wall: Thanks Mama, as always. Eagerly awaiting next week's share…

~

E lizza hadn't yet calmed herself down over the infuriating meeting she just had with Tarseen before she was confronted by the second thing that was bothering her that morning as soon as she opened the door and walked into the house.

"Elizza," her mother called. "Come to the kitchen when you put your things away. And change your clothes." The second sentence sounded more like a standalone command than a continuation of the first sentence. Suspicions were beginning to dawn, but she ruthlessly crushed them. Don't worry about disasters before they materialize, she quoted to herself. She dropped her purse on her bed, getting ready to remove her blazer. But then decided against it. *I might need it.*

She pushed the door open to the kitchen, and was unsurprised to find Kamaal sitting at the kitchen table, looking like he was there for an important meeting he arrived early for, afraid he might miss it. He's shaved recently, Elizza noted. His beard was long but had a trimmed quality it hadn't had since—just now. He smelled of too much cologne, and his hair was slicked back out of his face with some sort of gel or oil. *Libyan young men have two basic necessities in life, Elizza,* her father's words popped into her head unbidden. *Bread and hair gel.* She forgot to stop the smile blossoming on her face at the thought—she never would have suspected Kamaal of using hair gel! Unfortunately, she would recall the smile later that day as the source of Kamaal believing his words would be welcome.

∗∗∗

She, of course, had to disabuse him.

No, I would appreciate it if you didn't *talk to my dad. I am not interested.*

No, I don't think that being the wife of the imam of a VIP masjid is enough incentive to get me to change my mind.

No, I'm not worried about dying as an old, unmarried virgin. But thanks for your concern.

No, I'm not joking.

∗∗∗

She then had to sit in her room as her mother, who had just been supplied the news by Kamaal of Elizza's rejection, lectured her about refusing perfectly good offers of marriage. Apparently, a girl was not allowed to imagine the possibility of landing the man of her dreams.

"You're not pretty like your sister," her mother was saying, "and look how long it has taken her to find an acceptable man to show interest!" Elizza tried not to roll her eyes. "You can't afford to be picky. Your father is not going to be around forever and we want to see you settled before anything happens. To be comfortable. His salary does not stretch very far with you five girls. It is hard on him, and he is getting older. You have the opportunity to secure your future and put our hearts at ease. What do you have against Kamaal? He has a good job, is a hafidh, is well liked by everyone, wants to support you with school—"

"Mama, I just don't want to marry him," Elizza broke in. "He isn't someone I think I could be happy with."

"You didn't even give him a chance, didn't even consider accept-ing—"

"I've gotten to see how he is and the little I have seen is enough."

"You think you're going to get this amazing guy to become in-terested in you, a male model millionaire?" She admired her moth-er's alliteration, but couldn't help saying,

"Billionaire, Mama. You gotta account for inflation."

"Yes, you think someone with all of these qualities is just going to show up..." Her mother trailed off, looking at her second-oldest daughter in confusion. She could not internalize what was so objec-tionable about an offer from a mildly attractive, comfortably situated man of a similar age. Elizza looked back at her, seeing her mother's confusion but too weary to give explanations a try.

"It's no, Mama. That is my final answer. I won't change my mind."

***

Kamaal led the *fajr* prayer the next morning, as usual. He re-ally did have a heavenly voice, Elizza thought, before remembering to focus her concentration on prayer. When he said the final "*assa-laamu'alaikum*," he gave Elizza a wounded look over his left shoul-der. Her mother also looked her way, sending her a loaded, mean-ingful stare.

Elizza got ready for bed at 10 pm that night, having to wake up early to get ready for school the next morning, when she heard a knock on her door. She opened the bedroom door to her mother's face.

"Come," she said, leading Elizza to her room.

"Tell me your objections," she said, sitting on her bed and di-recting Elizza to sit on the edge. Elizza's heart sank. Her mother only ordered them to her room when they were in enormous trouble. Having her sit on the edge of the bed verged on nuclear disaster. To the rest of the world, she was an adult and shouldn't have to worry about getting in trouble with her mother. To her Libyan mother, she would never be too old for a good admonishment.

"Mama, I said no! You didn't make him think differently, did you?"

"I told him you needed to think about it and discuss with us. That's what you're doing."

"I don't need time."

"But tell me what you're looking for."

"Marriage is for life, Mama. Or, at least, that's supposed to be the intention."

"Don't lecture me about marriage like you know anything."

"I didn't mean—"

"Tell me," she interrupted. "What do you want in a husband exactly?" Elizza gave the question careful consideration for a few moments before replying.

"A good Muslim man who encourages me to do good—"

"Kamal is a *hafidh*," her mother cut in. Repeating the phrase for the umpteenth time.

"—and allows me to grow at my own pace!" Elizza finished. "Someone who supports my goals as if they were his own. Someone considerate of the needs of others. Educated. Good looking. A six pack would be nice," she ended with a laugh. Her mother swatted her arm.

She didn't have a very clear vision of her future as a married woman. She assumed she would get married one day—she did want kids, after all. She thought. They did look so adorable from far away, if a bit messy. And to a practicing Muslim woman, marriage was sort of a prerequisite to acquiring those. But what that would be like, look like, feel like, she couldn't really say. She did not have any close married friends, and her interactions with the opposite sex were pretty limited, her father having been stricter with her and Jana than her other sisters in terms of gender segregation, mostly just a result of following community norms. What a Muslim father was willing to allow in 2009 was vastly different than what he'd allow in 2019.

Ideally, she'd find a way to put her ideas into practice. To help people. And if she was honest about her ambition, to change the world. Improve Libya. Be an instrument of change. Her ideal husband, she supposed, would help her and enable her to carry out her goals and realize all of her dreams. He would certainly not stand in her way. She tried to convey all of that to her mother, but continually encountered a brick wall. The things she wanted seemed so far off of her mother's radar, she feared she could never make her really understand.

"You can't have everything, Elizza," her mother said finally. Umm ul'Banaat got up then, and walked out of the room. But the determined look in her mother's eyes let her know that whatever the outcome of this battle even was, the war was not over.

***

I see you, his expression seemed to say. The face, somehow, was cloudy, the features an unrecognizable blur, but the expression— clear as rain. *Your passion, your strength, your will—your self-discipline, your kindness, your empathy, your fury—your love. I see you. All your glory, through this tinted glass, and the thin streaks of almost invisible black, and all the varying shades of gray in your cloud of a soul, milky white if seen from a distance, but a shining, overwhelming orb of light if the viewer stops to look from just the right angle, enhanced by all of its depths and shades of color. I see you, my love.*

She blinked, rapidly, trying to make out the face, willing to see at least the color of those endlessly expressive eyes. The colors swayed, twirled, shifted, seemed to settle, on, was that an olive green? Her heart fluttered as she thought she recognized the face, before the color shifted again, to darken, and darken, and darken further, until she looked into eyes of intense midnight black. And then she woke up.

***

The next few weeks were a nightmare for Elizza. She could not have a single conversation with her mother that didn't end with her mother bringing up the dreaded Kamaal subject and accusing her of being an ungrateful daughter.

"I am not happy with you, Elizza," she said one day. "Daughters whose parents are upset with them will be cursed in life. A mother's *duaa* for her children is always answered, especially when she is *madhlooma.*" Elizza was home from school, in the kitchen helping her mother prepare dinner, and at that she almost spit out the water she took a sip of. Her mother, oppressed? As if she would ever let anyone! Elizza continued to slice onions, and if she began to cut them more aggressively thereafter, only she and the cutting board could know.

"Maybe you will share your *bazeen* recipe with me," she ventured as a peace offering the next day as her mother prepared dinner; it was technically not her day to help out, but she did not want to leave her mother too long to stew in her toxic ideas without adding a dash of the opposite view just to stir things up. Leedya was only too happy to let her take over.

"What use to you is any recipe?" her mother almost spat. "Get out of the kitchen! You will never need to cook because you will never get married! *Atla'i*! I won't share any of my recipes with a girl who will not marry someone her mother approves of!" Abu l'Banaat walked into the kitchen then, shooting his daughter a look of sympathy. "What can you make for the picnic next week?" he asked his wife. She looked confused, so he reminded her about the picnic to be held by BenAli and Tarseen the next weekend. In moments, she forgot Elizza, beaming brightly.

"Let's make a list of things to make. The girls can help me. Except Jana, she will need to get ready."

"Just for men," Abu l'Banaat emphasized.

"Just for men?" Umm ul'Banaat responded, unconcerned. "*Tawan shoofu.*" *We'll see about that.* Elizza wordlessly walked out and disappeared into her room.

***

When her mother heard that Kamaal was staying with Shayla's family for a visit soon, her attacks intensified.

"You *will* give him a chance!" she screamed at her daughter. "I spent too much effort on him last time to let this go to waste. We won't pay for your ticket to Libya when you visit your uncle if you don't. Your father will stop paying for your school if you do not sit with him." Elizza declined to mention that she was on scholarship— or that she already saved the money she would need for her ticket to Libya—didn't think it was the right time, or particularly helpful facts, to bring up. She simply replied,

"It would just be more waste of everyone's time, and prevent him from moving on and finding someone who actually *will* marry him, Mama."

Shayla arrived at just the right moment. Elizza had never been happier to see Shayla on her doorstep. Once they escaped to her room, she filled Shayla in on all the drama. Shayla was oddly reticent on the subject, instead commenting on marriage in general.

"What chance do we have of being happy if we have to just wait for the perfect guy to come ask for us?" Shayla asked. "My dad never lets us go around guys so not many even know we exist." Elizza grew silent, thinking of Jana. She hoped that BenAli eventually came and asked for her and turned out to be everything she wanted out of a husband. Jana needed the perfect guy—deserved him. She was such a delicate, sensitive girl. She was the kind of girl mothers wanted for their sons because they knew she'd be quiet and uncomplaining. Elizza smiled at the thought.

"We have to go find the perfect guy on our own. Then act like a Jana in front of his mom."

"Except my perfect man as a rule would *never* take advice about who to marry from his mom," Shayla sighed, taking her seriously.

"And mine wouldn't have a mom," Elizza replied, deadpan.

Chapter Ten

Shayla posted a photo, meme of woman ripping hair out. "Mood."

~

A few days later, Jana came upstairs accompanied by Shayla. Elizza smiled warmly. It was rare for Shayla to come over to their house two days in a row.

"*Salaam*! I didn't know you were coming." Shayla's smile in return was dim. "What's wrong?" she asked, standing up to pat her arm.

"I have to tell you…" Shayla trailed off, running her hand along the coverlet of Elizza's bed, then sitting down before standing straight up again and turning abruptly toward her. "I'm engaged." Elizza was floored. She didn't even know Shayla was talking to anyone about marriage. It all must have happened so fast. She didn't mention it during her last visit.

"Oh! Congratulations!" she said, after recovering from her shock. "Well, who's the lucky guy? Must have been a whirlwind romance," she tried some levity.

"It's Kamaal," Shayla said, maintaining her seriousness.

Elizza's mind drew a blank. "Kamaal who?" she asked dumbly. She only knew of one Kamaal that might be relevant here. Her mind refused to take it in.

"You know the one," Shayla said, her voice clipped. Elizza had to sit down.

"Do you need help?" she asked finally, in concern.

"I'll need help planning the wedding," Shayla said, deliberately misunderstanding. "Well, that's not entirely true. It's pretty much already been planned."

"What?" Elizza cried. "How—"

"Look," Shayla said. "I'll go into all of that later. It's not important. I just wanted to tell my best friend…my news," she finished lamely.

"Shayla, please. Just tell me how it happened. Is your mom…did your mom…?" Shayla cut her off again.

"No, not really. He asked for me, so I agreed to sit down and hear what he was looking for out of marriage and what he envisioned life would be like, and found we agreed on all of the day-to-day things that are important in a marriage."

"And what about…your nights?" Elizza pressed uncomfortably.

"He's pleasant enough to look at."

"Are you scared at all?" Shayla just gave her a look. Her fearless friend.

"Do you really think you can be happy?" she said finally. And seemed to hit a nerve.

"What makes you think I wouldn't be?" Shayla challenged, turning fully towards Elizza. "What makes you an expert on my happiness?"

"I just mean, if you were forced—" Elizza bit out. Shayla grew red.

"When was the last time you saw anyone successfully force me to do anything?" she demanded. Elizza thought hard. *Well, never.*

"I'm not some stupid pushover that would just stand aside and let someone else govern my life. You of all people should know me better than that." She met Elizza's gaze, a steady, fierce gleam in her eye, tinged with a sheen of tears she held back. "Your choices are not mine. Your lifestyle doesn't have to be mine. I'm sorry to get all emotional with you. I know it makes you uncomfortable. But I'm just telling you, if I have to deal with you looking at me with pity for the rest of my life, or marriage, I am not sure we can remain friends."

***

Elizza stayed laying down on her bed, staring at her ceiling long after Shayla left. She was starting to hate the idea of marriage. *She* didn't ever want to get married. Why? For what? From what she'd seen, it just made everyone miserable. Particularly women. They lost everything when they got married—most importantly, their independence. There was supposedly this new generation of Muslim men that were fine recognizing a woman's right to independence—for the price of taking on a man's responsibility. Cheap, right?

As long as she was willing to work full time, use her money to pay bills, take care of all household chores, spoil her husband, watch the kids, care for the kids, cook for the family, grocery shop, maintain the entire house, spend time with everyone, carefully budget expenses, she could go wherever she wanted. But just when, exactly, was she supposed to have the time?

***

Jana broke the news gently to her mom over dinner. Umm ul'Banaat stopped eating.

"They've been planning to get rid of Shayla for a while," she said at last. "The third *mindaar*. I knew she was keeping it for a reason." She continued eating, eerily quiet. The girls watched her cautiously, eating dinner in unprecedented silence. Their mother finished her food, left her plate on the table, and gave Elizza a deadly stare.

"You can clean up tonight," she said, and walked into the living room and picked up her cell phone.

"*Assalaamu'alaikum*, Fathiyah," she said into her phone, speaking to Shayla's mother, "what are we cooking for the engagement party?"

CHAPTER ELEVEN

Midwest Uni Emergency Team posted:

EMERGENCY ALERT: Reported sexual assault on University Blvd, Caucasian male in Navy hoody, approx. 5'11" tall at 19:00 Tuesday evening

~

The night sky winked down at her as she walked to class a few weeks later, normally a comforting friend, but today a cover of darkness—a cloak for nefarious activity. She felt jumpy and alert, thinking of the emergency text the university sent out to everyone just hours prior.

She still had two weeks until this half-semester class would be over, and she would be off to New York to help her friend with the wedding, not too much longer. But it would be sad for her too, because that would be the time that Shayla would be walking out of her life forever. Shayla was her closest friend, and now she would lose her to some imbecile who wouldn't be able to appreciate the amazing person she was. Elizza's sadness was so potent, she felt like someone she'd known had just died. Her heart twisted. Whenever she thought of Kamaal she could only think of him with enmity for having stolen something precious from her.

Shayla enlisted her exclusive help with the very few things that remained needing done for the wedding. But their relationship already felt strained. It was like Shayla had already passed on to the next phase of her life in her mind. A life where she wouldn't have much time for her single friend or where she refused to allow those friends to remind her—or convince her—of how unhappy she was. So Elizza helped her with the invitations and favors and quickly picking out a ready-made dress, even though she did it all with the sense that she was gnawing on the last bone she'd ever be thrown.

***

Elizza turned a corner, the eerie shadows giving her shivers as she glanced shiftily about. She tried to stay on the well-lit parts of the grounds at this late hour, but she was running late for her class and did not want to foster a reputation of tardiness with this particular teacher. She might want to ask him for a recommendation letter. Once she asked a professor to write her a recommendation letter for a scholarship and he remarked that he remembered she did well in his class—and that she was always late. Not a good impression to leave behind. Especially if the professor was inclined to be literal and honest on his recommendation letters. "Despite her habitual tardiness to my class, consequently resulting in her missing crucial sections of lectures she would need to hear in order to succeed on the exams that I administered, Ms. Elizza performed surprisingly well in my class and surpassed all others in her intellectual answers to exam questions..."

Elizza amused herself drafting the honest-to-a-fault professor's recommendation letter, but snapped quickly out of it when she saw the shadow of a tall man approaching her on the sidewalk. She reached into her pocket and clenched her fingers around her Mace bottle, curving her finger to fit over the spray nozzle in readiness, her heart racing. The overbright screen of a cell phone illuminated the face of her potential assailant, and she almost breathed a sigh of relief before other of her wary instincts fell into place. He looked up, and stopped abruptly.

"Hey. I mean, *Assalaamu'alaikum*," said Tarseen.

"Walaikum assalaam," Elizza responded warily, resuming her quick strides in the direction of her class. A few seconds later, she could hear him quicken his own steps to keep up.

"What brings you to this part of campus?" he asked, for all the world as if this was his home campus and not hers.

"I have a class to get to," she said, the last word an octave higher than the rest of the sentence. Wasn't it obvious? She dug her hands further into her coat pockets and walked faster. He matched his steps to hers.

"Wow, this is a late hour to have a class." Elizza did not respond. "But then again, it goes get dark early these days." Still no response. "Does it make you nervous, walking to class in the dark alone?"

"You mean, am I afraid I will be bothered by tall male strangers on my way?"

He smiled slightly. "Something like that."

She smiled even wider. "No, not really," she lied. "It's a busy campus and I keep my Mace on hand for emergencies." He nodded his head slowly, as if bowing to her wise decision. They walked side by side quietly for some time, despite Elizza's attempts to walk at a different pace. For some reason, he would not budge. He would not talk either, so instead of making the walk to her class go faster, it became an interminable period of time. "So what brings *you* to this part of campus?" she asked.

"I have a talk," he said, after a pause.

"And you're not afraid of walking alone in the dark?" she asked, her face all innocent smile.

"No," he said quickly. "I am a black belt in Judo." She perked up in interest.

"Really?"

"No," he said, just as quickly, his smile sheepish. "Not at all. I don't even carry a weapon so I'm even less protected than you are. But I figure my size and height will probably scare most people away." Wow, who knew he could crack a joke? she thought. They continued walking. More silence. And then Tarseen abruptly broke it, uttering,

"Hey, would you—do you—?" But he cut himself off abruptly. He seemed distracted and torn.

"What?" Elizza said finally, impatient. He looked at her face for a few seconds before shaking his head.

"I can't remember what I was going to ask," he said finally, his face going cold. "Some suggestion for your plan, I think." She eyed him skeptically. But then her building came into view.

"Well, gotta go. *Salaam*," she said quickly, and disappeared into the building.

***

Elizza thought that would be the last time she'd ever have to walk to her building along Tarseen's side. But the next time she had her evening class, he intercepted her yet again on her way. Again, he didn't talk much, just sent absent, blank stares in her direction, and continued along the same path, not walking with her exactly, but walking a few steps behind. Much like the distance a manservant would follow behind his mistress back in the day, she thought with amusement. She could see Tarseen wearing a dark servant's tuxedo, white cravat starched, climbing up to touch the end of his close shaven beard. He might actually look handsome dressed like that, she mused, if only he would smile once in a while—and weren't such a jerk.

"You know," she said, before she walked into the building. "I always take this path to class. Because it's the shortest way." Dot dot dot. He did not *have* to keep running into her. Hopefully he would get the hint.

CHAPTER TWELVE

Tyler Parker
to Firas Tarseen<tarseen.1@midwestuni.edu>.
Subject: Class yesterday

Dear Professor Tarseen,

Please excuse my absence from class yesterday afternoon. I got into a car accident on my way over and was unable to make it, or let you know in advance. Thank you and see you next class.

-Tyler Parker
Sophomore
Midwest Uni

Firas Tarseen
to Tyler Parker<parker.109@midwestuni.edu>
Subject: RE: Class Yesterday

Really? That's odd. Your friend told me you blew off my class to go skydiving.

-Firas Tarseen, CEO
SmartLy Constructed, Inc.

~

"What did you get up to last night?" George Wi'am said in lieu of greeting, seeing her sitting at her accustomed place in the Panera café. *We have to stop meeting like this*, she wanted to say. But of course, didn't. She sort of enjoyed the personal attention, but disliked it too. She didn't want anyone passing by to get the wrong impression of her.

"Just had class," she said evasively.

"I think I saw you walking there," he said. "I think it was you that was walking with Firas Tarseen." She blushed at the implication, and the tone, of his words.

"I wasn't walking with him," she immediately denied.

"He was trailing you like a lost puppy," he retorted. She rolled her eyes, trying to decide what to say. She hardly knew why they kept having to walk together herself. She certainly didn't *want* to.

"He just teaches a class that way," she said. "We just end up intercepting each other most evenings." George shot her a sympathetic smile.

"No, he doesn't teach a class there," he informed her.

"Yes, he does." She paused. "He said he does."

"It wouldn't be the first time he lied about something."

"What? How do you even know?" Elizza demanded. *And why is this your business?*

"Look—I'm telling you from experience. Don't trust him. He's bad news. People who grow up with privileged backgrounds think nothing of trampling all over the little guys. They're ruthless when it comes to taking the things they want."

"What does that have to do with me? I don't have anything valuable."

"You don't have any ideas he might want to steal from you?" That gave her pause.

"But you said he doesn't have a class there. How do you know?"

"Because I looked up his schedule at the beginning of the semester so I could avoid seeing his face. He doesn't even teach a class on Wednesdays." She vowed to look it up herself, but stayed silent, thinking.

"So what did he do to you?" she asked quietly, almost afraid of the answer. He stared at her, assessing—deciding.

"Okay, I'll tell you," he said finally, sitting down across from her. "But I don't want this getting around."

***

The allegations were wild. Tarseen's family were all Gaddafi supporters, and profited from their connections with the dictator by accepting government contracts for building projects, and spending only half of the money given them on the actual project. A common enough occurrence, Elizza supposed. She heard of lots of people becoming rich that way—people with the worst sort of reputations in the "not rich" segment of the expat Libyan community, those who were able to immigrate to the United States by virtue of their bad experiences and likely torture by Gaddafi forces if they ever returned to Libya—before the dictator was removed from power. It was not an unbelievable story, really, but she never heard anyone mention it before. But then again, maybe it was an unknown fact. George seemed to have a previous connection with the family that made him privy to all sorts of their family drama.

The bulk of which held no interest for her whatsoever. There were some sort of marriage schemes that took place within the family to make sure that they married first or second cousins, to keep the wealth all in the family, according to George. She had to interrupt him several times to get him back on point. After all, he started this conversation telling her that Tarseen did something awful to him. She wanted to hear about *that.*

As it happened, George's father profited directly from those alleged government contracts, a fact that George glossed over, as exclusive subcontractor to the Tarseen family construction business. George and Tarseen saw each other all the time, as sons of semi-business partners and close friends—their fathers studied as engineers at the same university in the United States. They got to travel with their fathers on their business trips around the world, and were homeschooled by the same tutor, paid for by Tarseen's father.

"Tarseen's dad always planned to give his son the business," he said. "So he wanted him to learn it all from an early age."

"And your dad?"

George smiled ruefully. "Wanted to keep me out of trouble." But he didn't go into detail, only added, "He didn't have a great relationship with my mom, after he converted to Islam. Eventually they got divorced and my mom moved back to Lebanon and got remarried, and he had no one to look after me when he went out of the country." Elizza nodded, feeling a bit sorry for him about the semi-loss of a parent at a young age, and George continued with his story.

"My father passed away, and it turned out that he didn't leave me any money because he was under a mountain of debt that my mom racked up, and was funneling everything he had to try to pay it off. He almost finished paying it off before he died. But that left me as a young man with no money, no family or other resources in Libya, and only the Tarseen family to help me out. So Tarseen's dad promised to pay for my school. But he never wrote it down or documented it or anything. He died soon after my own father. Got hit by a block of cement some worker carelessly dropped when he was building. When I started applying for schools here in the United States, and went to the son with an acceptance letter and a tuition statement, he refused to pay it."

"But isn't he super rich?"

"Yes. Very. But the thing about rich men, Elizza, is that they can be the stingiest, greediest type of people."

***

Later that day, Elizza sorted through the checks for their local family charity as part of her community service, having volunteered her accounting services to help the nonprofit organization. But she couldn't help thinking about what George said about Tarseen. *Is it true?* she kept asking herself. She wasn't sure, though, why someone like George would just make something like that up. Let alone decide she was the person to tell it to. And he told her not to let it get around. He seemed to just be putting her on her guard. She remembered explaining her business plan to him the last time he met—he seemed to think it was a good idea. Unlike some people.

Or maybe Tarseen just wanted her to *think* he thought it wouldn't work?

She just wasn't sure. George was such a nice guy, it was hard to see him making up something like that about another person. And Tarseen was so full of himself and condescending, she could definitely see him thinking nothing of cheating someone out of several thousands of dollars—he probably didn't even realize how devastating doing something like that to someone could be. What was that amount of money to a millionaire?

She tried to focus on the task before her, opening envelopes and writing the donation amounts down in the credit column of the accounting book. It was nice to see people unexpectedly give money to these causes. There were, of course, the big names that basically funded the local Muslim organizations—Dr. Control Freak, board member on every board that existed. Brother Secretly Rich, lives in a small nondescript home with his quiet family, all of them frequent mosque visitors. Mrs. Bored Housewife, likes to donate when she can't think of other things on which to spend her rich husband's money.

Then there were the surprises—owners of local alcohol selling Carry-Outs, donating the odd $2,000 or $5,000. She liked to picture them—okay, romanticize them—as they wrote out their checks, maybe from office rooms of their large houses, looking over their children. She pictured a man zeroing in his son as he played—the one with the mental incapacity—tears forming in his eyes as he fondly watches him flying the drone he bought him with his *haram* or illegitimately earned money, and then bending down to fill out a page in his checkbook, whispering, "Allah forgive me," over it as he signs it and seals it away in an envelope.

She opened the next check and whistled at the figure. $10,000. Wow big spender, she thought, Mister… she read the name at the top of the check. Firas Tarseen. She blinked. *Show off*, she thought. Then she saw the enclosed pledge and receipt form.

Can we publish your donation to encourage others to emulate your generosity?
☐YES ☑NO

Okay, maybe not a showoff, she conceded. But he's still a jerk. And what a fortunate thing to come across—if that didn't prove her point about him not understanding the value of money to the everyday little person, she didn't know what did.

***

The first thing she did when she got home that day was tell Jana everything George told her. Okay, he said don't tell anyone, but telling the story to someone as closed-mouthed as Jana didn't really count.

Jana was bewildered.

"My gosh, Elizza. That's really sad," she finally said. "Poor guy. It must have been hard on him to lose his father and then his only solid connection to Libya at the time."

"Yeah. I can't imagine."

"And to think he would at least have some money to live on and find out he couldn't count on anything to build his future with. That's rough. For a guy living in Libya, having nothing to start with makes it impossible to build their futures."

"Yeah. And only the worst monster would ever put him in such a situation."

"But *alhamdulillah*, at least he had his U.S. citizenship. He is a citizen, I'm assuming? Or did he come as a student…?"

"No, he was born here when his dad was studying. Tarseen too, he said. But that's not the point. Even coming here doesn't make his situation any less awful." Jana stared at her pink quilted coverlet thoughtfully.

"Maybe Tarseen didn't know his dad promised George the money," she said finally. "To him it could have seemed like George asking for a handout."

"No, he said Tarseen knew about it. And even if he didn't, he could have at least given him *something* to help him out. Whatever his coffers could spare at the time." Jana smiled at her vehemence.

"Maybe he didn't have enough cash—what's that called?"

"—liquid assets—"

"Yeah, liquid assets at the time to help."

Elizza sighed in exasperation. "I don't buy that! You can't be a successful international businessman without a healthy amount of liquidity." Jana looked unconvinced, the distant expression still across her face.

"And he sent a $10,000 check to family services today," she blurted. "You only send that much when you have a comfortable amount of cash. He could start paying for his school *now* even if he didn't have enough then."

"Wow," Jana said, her eyes widening. "Ten *thousand* dollars? That was really generous."

"Yeah—if only his generosity extended to people he is obligated to help, too," Elizza responded.

"Elizza, we really don't know the whole story. We shouldn't just make assumptions about people when we can never actually know the entire story."

"Gosh, Jana, stop with the excuses. It's a terrible story, isn't it? Admit that at least. Or are you calling George a liar?"

"We're supposed to make seventy excuses for our Muslim brothers and sisters. It's *sunnah*."

"*We* aren't the ones wronged here, so that's not our job." Jana raised an eyebrow at her.

"You want me to call Maryam in here so we can ask her?" she offered with a smile. Elizza laughed.

"No no. Okay, you win. But at least admit, if that is what happened, only the worst *monster* could do something like that."

Jana's face fell. "It is a really sad thing for a Muslim man to ever do to his brother in Islam. I really hope it's not true."

CHAPTER THIRTEEN

Firas Tarseen edited a post:

Libyan Men's Family* Picnic this Saturday

At Memorial Park
3 pm to park close (sunset)

There's been a slight change of plans.

Sorry for overlooking you before, ladies. You're welcome to attend, too.

~

There should be a lot to say about this event, but we only really care about the highlights, don't we? And they are:

BenAli, secretly thrilled that Umm ul'Banaat infiltrated her way into the event and made sure that it would include women, did his utmost to run into and talk to Jana at every opportunity. His heart swelled when he saw her, and her face turned the most endearing shade of pink at every encounter. He was nearly sure she was *the one*.

Kamaal made a show of fussing over his new fiancé, bringing her plates of food and dessert, and ignoring Elizza sitting next to her steadfastly. Shayla ended up leaving early, saying she was getting a headache.

Leedya and Kawthar did what they always did at events where they would encounter single and eligible young Libyan men—pretend to studiously ignore them while doing everything they possibly could to draw their attention.

Maryam did not attend.

Umm ul'Banaat rotated the tables like a hummingbird gathering nectar from a field of flowers, alternatively gossiping with the matrons and spreading the good news of her daughter's soon-to-be good fortune.

Abu l'Banaat alternated watching people in amusement and socializing, mostly with the younger men.

And Elizza sat somewhat forlornly at a table with a distracted Jana, after Shayla left, and some other young Libyan girls, not saying or eating much, feeling sad about her friend, feeling sad that her sister would probably be moving on with life too. And she had the sense that Tarseen was avoiding looking her way or being in her proximity whatsoever. Until George arrived.

"How are you doing?" George asked her, suddenly appearing next to her at the food table, filling his plates with heaps of food.

She was happy to see him. She thought. She was a little distracted at the moment. Still wondering about his Tarseen story, trying to gauge their reactions to each other.

George cleared his throat awkwardly. She blushed. She forgot to pay attention to what he asked.

"Good, *alhamdulillah*," she answered finally. It was nice, after all, to have those dreamy green eyes trained on her for the moment. Seconds later, however, she noticed another pair of eyes perk up to peer in her direction, and watch their interaction studiously. She finished exchanging pleasantries with George in a distracted fashion, until she saw movement in her peripheral vision, and saw Tarseen exit the building, the door closing swiftly behind him.

Chapter Fourten

MSM from Kareema

Salaam, sry we cant come 4 a last visit. My brother doesn't have any more classes n wants to leave ASAP so he can focus on business. Tarseen needs him to clean up some mess in NYC. Looks like we wont see u again 4 a while. Well miss u! come visit if youre ever in NYC! Salaam Lovely!

~

A few days later, the girls were sitting in the living room watching a movie (except Maryam, who was of the opinion that movies were *haram*). They were all enjoying themselves, sharing popcorn and boxes of $0.98 candy from Walmart when Jana got up quickly and disappeared from the room, but not before Elizza saw her stricken expression. Not wanting to alert any of her other family members, she waited a few minutes before following her out.

"Jana, what's wrong?" she asked, closing the door to their room softly behind her. Jana wordlessly handed her her phone, its screen open to a newly received text message.

Elizza's read it quickly, her heart sinking more after each word, but she did her best to school her expression.

"Okay, so he isn't going to be around here anymore. Doesn't mean he doesn't want you."

***

She was glad they were gone for her own sake, but sad for her sister. Jana had such hopes of an amazing romantic union, escaping the cloying expectations of her mother, into something much more comforting and brighter. Elizza had no idea what the reason for BenAli's sudden departure from the scene was, and could only be sorry for it. But she was relieved his odd friend would no longer be around, watching her with his judgmental eyes, thinking he was better than everyone and everything in his path.

And now she had the wedding to contend with. Why her friend insisted she be there to help with the preparations was a mystery with such a big family already there to help her out. Some odd olive branch, if that was what it was. Still, she was determined to be there for her friend as she started out this new chapter of her life, however ill-judged Elizza thought her decision was. It was the Spring season, and the Spring of the start of Shayla's life, full of hope and budding emotions and the excitement of warmth after the frost. If anyone could make something with such ingredients, Shayla could.

Hopefully Jana could get through the week of spring break without Elizza there to comfort her. Jana always had a sentimental and sensitive disposition. She tended to take disappointments more to heart than any of her other sisters. It always took her a while to overcome setbacks. She could also not hear about the misfortunes of others without it affecting her mood. Elizza could always tell the days that something was going on with one of Jana's students at the daycare. Jana would be so lost in thought that conversations became painful—if not impossible. During Libya's 2011 war, Jana was an absolute wreck, reading the news avidly for any hint that something may have happened to a friend or family member over there.

When they were younger, Elizza, though fiercely protective of her sister, would sometimes grow weary of such emotional indulgence. In ways, Jana's emotional tendencies reminded her of her mother, and sort of irritated her. Her reaction became to tamp down her own emotions, and to downplay any bad news she had to deliver. Nowadays, she wondered if Jana had an undiagnosed depressive disorder—although she would never in a million years suggest such a thing to her mother, who would waste no time forcing her docile older daughter to undergo all the *sehr* and *'ain* cures she could get the local imam to perform. Then again, with the loss of her daughter's suitor, she might just get the local imam to perform them, anyway.

***

Umm ul' Banaat was having a bad week. First, she loses Elizza's future husband to Fathiyah's daughter, of all people. Now, Jana had lost her beau.

Elizza's mom was walking through the house, waving a stick of incense. Elizza walked through a cloud of its smoke as she came down the stairs to eat a quick dinner before leaving for class. She paused in front of the kitchen door, wondering what her mom was up to.

Umm ul'Banaat spotted her and waved the incense her way. Elizza fanned the air in front of her face and coughed.

"Mama!"

"I'm protecting our family from *ain*," she said. "You need to let it reach you, too. I should have kept quiet about Jana! Who knows how many people gave her '*ain* and now look what happened." Elizza just shook her head and took cover in the kitchen, hoping that when she was older, she wouldn't inherit her mother's crazy.

She needed to check Twitter—she would get the latest news about Libya sooner from there than anywhere else, and she was worried about the trip to Libya she was planning for the summer. She quickly scrolled the feeds of people who usually retweeted the latest news. The situation seemed to have settled down of late. She would tell her father, or reassure him really. He kept his own eye on the news as well but his news sources were mainly: actual news websites, and Facebook; the former was outdated by the time it was actually written, and Libyan news sources from the latter source either hadn't heard of the term "verified," or widely misused it. The Boy Who Cried Wolf had maxed out his cries for help during the last Tripoli war. She finished her updates on what was happening in Libya and was getting ready to close the app—she could only let herself go so far into her feed before she knew she would get reeled in for far longer than she'd intended—when she came across the following exchange between her little sisters:

Who's That Pretty Girl? @LeedyaLeebiyyah: Check out @LibyanStrongMan's new pics. He is 🔥

@ThatRiverInHeaven: @LeedyaLeebiyyah @LibyanStrongMan Did you mean lit or hot? 😏

@LeedyaLeebiyyah: 🖤 You ruined it. But… both lol
@SomeRandomLibyanGirl: @ThatRiverInHeaven
@LeedyaLeebiyyah @LibyanStrongMan You're right, tho…
yummmm

Elizza continued to scroll. It only got worse from there. Bandwagons of other girls, Libyan and non-Libyan, joined the thread with their own comments, so that within twenty or so tweets about the subject, what started out as blatant appreciation of male physical perfection soon downward spiraled into downright stalking. She had to stop herself after a few minutes of reading—she didn't think she could handle much more of it. She only knew of one word to describe the sad little thread, if only she could think of it. What is that word the young kids used these days? Oh yeah. *Thirsty.*

What is wrong with teenagers these days? she wondered. Then she wondered if all teenagers were that…thirsty. And then still wondered what her sisters were thinking. Did they think that was cute? Poor things, she thought, they probably did. Well, she had to be going, but, because her "I'm not their parent" mantra was getting stale and unconvincing by now, couldn't help screaming,

"Leedya! Kawthar! You know your Twitter comments are *public,* right?" before walking out the door to go to class.

***

On her walk to class a light drizzle greeted her. She pulled up her hood to keep away the worst of the drops. She was terrible at remembering to carry an umbrella. She blinked her eyes several times to get the rain drops off of her eyelashes, and when she opened them again, to her chagrin she saw Tarseen approaching her from the side.

"I thought you guys left," she said abruptly, forgetting to say *salaam.* "Kareema was kind enough to send us a message to let us know you were all leaving."

"I have a few more things to do before I go," he said shortly. "Some more classes and things."

"Is he—" Elizza began, but corrected herself. "Are you guys planning to visit here again? Anytime soon?"

"Not sure," he said. "We don't have any plans to at the moment." She wanted to ask about BenAli specifically, but was put off by Tarseen's cold manner. She was burning on the inside. She wanted to ask why he let his friend lead Jana on, and how he could treat George like a relentless beggar when they practically grew up like brothers.

"So why is it you keep walking to your class everyday?" she asked instead, irritably. "Don't they give you guys special parking classes so you don't set bad examples for your students and show up late?"

"I like the walk," he said, after a pause. He was wearing a suave dress jacket with no hood, gripping a small compact umbrella tightly in his hand as he walked.

"It's raining," she said, drawing out the sentence.

"Rain is…healthy for you," he replied. "It restores your natural vibrations." He swallowed visibly. She regarded him quizzically over her shoulder as he avoided eye contact, noting his usually tamed hair springing into wild-ish curls from the rain—and subsequently tripped over a tennis shoe left carelessly on the sidewalk. She looked away embarrassed, but when she regarded him again, he pretended not to notice. Pretended she was not there, more like.

The rest of their walk continued in silence. When she reached her building, the rain intensified, so she said a quick *salaam* and turned away, when she heard him yell, "Wait!"

When she turned around, he approached quickly and stuffed something into her hands, muttering, "I don't know *why* you don't carry one of these," before turning around to run off in another direction. Not to a class, if George was to be believed. She looked down to see what he had given her. It was his umbrella.

She did not run into him by accident at the university again, because that was the last day of her half semester evening class.

Chapter Fifteen

Hajja Khadijah posted on NY Muslim Culture Association page:

I keep seeing ladies bringing their kids in the main musallah for jumaa. Ladies, we have two separate rooms for women with children to sit with their kids in, so kindly utilize them and let those without kids have a chance to hear what the khateeb is saying. Jazakum Allah khair.

~

Before she knew it, spring break had arrived. But Elizza couldn't enjoy her break, because that was the week she promised to Shayla, to come to New York to help her with wedding preparations.

"Just be forewarned," Shayla said, as Elizza sat in the waiting area of the airport, waiting to board her flight. "We will be dealing mainly with Hajja Khadijah."

Who was Hajja Khadijah? Shayla would just explain.

Hajja Khadijah was the founder and main benefactress of the local masjid of Kamaal's community, the masjid at which Kamaal was the salaried imam, personally selected by her. She single-handedly contributed the initial funds to build the masjid in their community, and then raised funds to complete it. She was overheard to say the masjid was "for doctors and lawyers, no less." Elizza wondered where her community college professor father's place on that hierarchy was—several rungs beneath wealthy beyond reason widow and multimillion-dollar international business owner, no doubt. She was a permanent board member of the masjid, made sure to have the bylaws indicate that fact, and kept an eye on every detail, from the subject matter of the youth halaqas to the events that were sponsored by the social committee. No matter was too small to require her input.

If she did not have a hand in something that went on at the masjid, it would by default not meet with her satisfaction. No one could do things as well as she could.

Hajja Khadijah was known as a pious woman in their community. She was known to strictly adhere to (her own strict interpretation of) *sharia* in every respect. She never left the house without a mahram, and required that her several nephews come for extended visits regularly so that she always had someone to chauffeur her around when needed. She had a ton of money, of course, being one of the beneficiaries of her enormously wealthy father's will.

All of this, Shayla explained to her over the phone, before breaking to Elizza that Hajja Khadijah would be with her when she picked up her friend from the airport.

"Oh…and she wants to take us out to lunch," she added, almost apologetically.

***

These are the thoughts that were running through Elizza's mind all throughout lunch:

Should I offer to pay the bill when it comes? Hajja Khadijah ordered at least two separate meals.

Shayla is so nervous she can barely even swallow her food.

As intrusive and interfering as the Hajja is, you have to admire a lady that can inspire so many people to cower.

Maariyah is adorable. She's trying so hard not to say anything aib *that she can't think of anything at all to say. I can't think of a single time she kept so silent. She normally dominates conversations!*

Elizza walked out of the restaurant in relief.

"Oh, I forgot to pick up Shayla's henna dress from the seamstress!" she had said, smacking her forehead in a way she hoped didn't look too theatrical. What she really meant to do was escape by any means necessary. She had endured an interrogation more difficult than anything she would be asked at her business plan defense at the end of the school year, she had no doubt. Nothing seemed off limits to that woman—her education, her family, her family's income, the price of their house!

She spotted the car she was driving—Kamaal's car as a loan—across the street, and hoped she put enough money in the parking meter. Shayla had kindly allowed her to escape, assuring her she would get a ride back to the house with the Hajja.

A familiar looking man was sitting in a car parallel parked on the curb by the restaurant. *Is that Tarseen?* She wondered, doing a double take. *It is. What in the world is he doing here?*

***

What is she doing here? Tarseen wondered. He noticed that she had actually stopped to stare, and then snapped out of it and continued walking. For a few seconds, he engaged in a fierce mental battle with himself. And then found himself losing the battle, opening the door to his car and standing up before she made it to the crosswalk.

"Elizza," he said, in lieu of greeting.

"Tarseen," she responded. He held back a smile—the scene reminded him of enemies greeting each other in the movies. She seemed to eye him warily. He tried not to be overfriendly.

"What brings you here?" he asked.

"My best friend's wedding," she said shortly. "I assume you're here as a guest too? A little early though, isn't it? Or are you the best man?" He laughed.

"I am my aunt's chauffeur for the week," he replied. He tried to keep the annoyance out of his voice. It was a trial coming to visit his aunt. He tried to give her her due respect, if for no other reason than to honor his father's memory. But she made things overly difficult on herself and others by refusing to drive.

Elizza stood there silently, looking like she wanted to run. But she looked sort of forlorn, too. Then he remembered that Shayla was a close friend of hers, and had the sense that she did not keep many people close to her.

"You're going to miss your friend," he said abruptly. She nodded slowly, looking a question at him. "You can always come visit her again," he commented, aiming for a consoling tone. She just looked angry.

"If I could afford the air fare every weekend," she retorted, "that might make me feel better."

"I'm sure her family will visit her sometimes," he said. "Maybe you can come up with them. I'm sure she will miss them."

"She is choosing to leave everyone behind," Elizza said resentfully, almost forgetting who she was talking to, caught up in her subject.

"You wouldn't want to do that yourself," he responded softly. "Would you?" She blinked in confusion. What were they talking about again? He stepped back and looked at his watch awkwardly.

"Well, I have a call," he said abruptly, before dismissing her and getting back into his car, pulling his phone out of his pocket.

Chapter Sixteen

Kamaal BenTaleb changed his relationship status to, "Married."

Kamaal BenTaleb tagged Elizza BenTaleb in a post.

~

The day of the wedding *finally* dawned. For Elizza, it was too long coming. She wanted it to be over with. She was bone weary, and still sad that her friend would be moving far away. She needed time to process it all—but didn't have the time what with all of the preparations she was helping with.

The effect of the banquet hall was overwhelmingly extravagant. This was the wedding of their esteemed imam, as Hajja Khadijah was quick to let everyone know. So everyone in the community was invited to come celebrate, give the couple gifts, and promise to be involved with all future events at the local masjid. They had a small Libyan community in that section of New York, so several families were imported in from other cities, mostly others in New York but such was the illustriousness of Hajja Khadijah, there were at least a dozen and a half that flew in from other states. Elizza's family could not make it because the cost of flights were too high for all seven members—and Umm ul'Banaat was still too bitter about Shayla's marriage to insist upon it with her husband. Elizza nodded to the few families that had flown in from their town, although Shayla's family hadn't had much time to send out invitations to their friends. The truth of the matter was, the wedding they were all attending was planned for another woman. No one knew, of course, except for Hajja Khadijah, Shayla's family, and Elizza—and Shayla only filled her in on that crucial detail the day she arrived in New York. But

Kamaal was suffering from a broken engagement when he landed on Umm and Abu l'Banaat's doorstep, and was probably on the rebound from that failed relationship. In addition, he was desperate to replace her with another woman rather than cancel the wedding plans that had been several months in the making, and lose the deposits he'd already paid for the venue and catering. Shayla's acceptance mended his broken heart, maintained the status quo of his pocketbook, and last but certainly not least, helped him save face in front of the community. Hajja Khadijah was also instrumental in helping with that last thing—she crushed any hints of rumors about a former engagement with brutal force.

The Libyan traditions were followed to a T in keeping with their heritage. The day before had been the henna party, and Hajja Khadijah played the part of Shayla's mother-in-law, as Kamaal's family was unable to obtain visas to attend the wedding due to the federal travel ban. She placed the circle of henna onto Shayla's hand with the possessiveness of a woman who's son was actually getting married that day. Elizza watched the scene with some qualms for her friend that she decided not to voice—*too late now*, she thought, and winced as she remembered the last time she'd tried to question Shayla's choice.

Today was the main wedding event, *laylat ad-dukhla*. The next day would be the *aseeda* day, *subhiyat al-irs*, the morning after breakfast. Elizza was so tired she only hoped she wouldn't sleep through her alarm the following morning.

She was starting to feel like a paperboy. It was hard to enjoy the wedding, because each moment she was required by Hajja Khadijah to fetch something new –for the bride, for a guest. She caught snatches of conversations as she passed tables.

"Your new daughter-in-law dances well," one lady commented to the woman next to her. The supreme compliment. To dance is to put yourself on display and invite commentary on your abilities. Also your weight, your skin color, your hair, your clothes, your carriage, your confidence, and any other thought that crosses the mind of any of your observers. It can be hard to truly dance for the joy of it under such circumstances. Unless you have been to enough of these events to have gotten used to it, or even to have forgotten what is taking place as you swing your hips with abandon. Which, to be fair, many of the ladies had. Elizza watched the women dance wistfully.

She smiled as she heard ladies at another table discussing their own weddings. The married ladies' most cherished topic of conversation at weddings was—revisiting the grandeur of their weddings. But to be fair, this was a topic that could be brought up on any occasion, and to which most, if not all, the married women could contribute and loved to wax eloquent on whenever the opportunity presented itself.

Hajja Khadijah spotted her as she walked to the table where she kept her purse to grab Shayla her lipstick.

"Ayesha wants a glass of diet Coca Cola," she informed Elizza. She made her way to the alcohol-free bar at the back of the banquet hall—apparently the waiter had accidentally given the lady a regular Coca Cola. She approached the table from behind Hajja Khadijah, balancing the overly full cup in her hands, and could not help overhearing an interesting conversation taking place. She stopped just short of joining the table, conveniently camouflaged by a tall potted tree with lights placed near a wall of the hall (although she did not consider herself to be hiding—she was merely taking a short break before actually delivering the goods. Even servants were allowed breaks every once in a while!).

"Tarseen's friend, that BenAli," Hajja Khadijah was saying, "he is his business partner. They're like brothers. Met at university. Tarseen was telling me how he saved him from a disastrous marriage." She waited for her tablemates to ask her for details. Shayla's mom looked nervously around her, ensuring no one could hear the conversation that probably shouldn't. Elizza ducked further behind the tree.

"A mother was after a rich man for her daughter. She would do anything to get her married. Tarseen was afraid her mother wouldn't even leave her a choice. See, that's why I believe rich men need to marry a close family friend or distant relative so they can be sure of the family's intentions. That's why Tarseen's mother and I agreed on a match between my Anaya and him."

Elizza's heart beat fast, but she had too much to do to process the information. The spot of a grudge on her heart, formerly nursed to a small seedling, had lain dormant for a while, slowly dying with the passage of time. But now it flowered with a new vengeance, and even though her mind was not free to contemplate or digest the information, her emotions boiled in a steamy rage she vowed to nurse later that evening. When she had a free moment. Maybe at 5 am.

***

"Elizza, Kamal texted me to ask us to send them a *darbooka*," Shayla said, a dumbfounded look on her face. "Didn't we…?"

"I think I put one on their side," she said.

"They can't find it anywhere. Here, take ours to the storeroom for someone to pick up, but see if you can find theirs first. I don't want to be without one." Elizza picked up the women's *darbooka* and donned her abaya and hijab before walking out of the ballroom, frankly relieved to get away and ponder what she heard. Tarseen chased his friend away from Jana? She was incensed, but hardly surprised. It seemed he had ruining people's lives worked out to an art form. She took out her phone to check for messages from Jana, her heart wrenching again for the cruel end to her sister's dreams.

Elizza: How are you doing?
Jana: Im ok, thx

She sighed as she swung the door of the storeroom inward, wanting to climb into her phone and come out through her sister's to give her a real hug. But seconds later, she was the one in need of a hug. She halted in the doorway of the storeroom as she came face to face with Tarseen.

Chapter Seventeen

"I'm supposed to find a *darbooka* for you guys?" Elizza said, uncomfortable. *Of all the men to run into,* she thought, annoyed.

"Kamaal sent me to—" he began, then stopped, his speech halted. He paced. Started to speak again and then paused. Elizza watched him warily, taking in his agitated appearance in confusion. His black tuxedo, impeccable but with a bowtie that was askew, as if he had fidgeted it out of place. His hair, however, was somehow miraculously still tamed in a stylish look, with his hair halved into two unequal parts, one side of it taller than the other. His hands alternated their position on his person—they started out in his pockets. Then he crossed them over his chest. Back to his pockets. Cradling the back of his neck with his elbows winged out, like he was getting ready to do some lunges. Elizza was almost amused, but she *really* didn't have time for this. She pulled the sleeve of her black abaya away from her wrist to look at the designer watch she picked out as an accessory to the shimmery gold dress she wore—not so much to check the time as show her impatience.

"No, not really. He didn't send me," he admitted, finally turning to look at her, staring down at his hands for a second like he didn't know *what* to do with them before stuffing them into his pockets. "I sent myself." Another pause. Now he had her attention. She stared dumbly, then looked at the floor in embarrassment, remembering how much makeup she'd directed the beautician at the mall to put on her face—a treat she was able to sneak in when Shayla asked her to pick up a color of lipstick she was running out of. "I needed to talk to you." He paced uneasily. "I had him text his wife to send you." She just waited for him to go on. *This is strange,* was the only thought she could pick out of the jumble of things that were passing through her head. The other things were indecipherable, because most of them were just particles of blind rage.

"I had to talk to you," he repeated, in justification. "It's been hard deciding to tell you this. So many reasons not to… You're … outspoken, and … your family is a train wreck, and—"

"Excuse me?" she cried, startled out of her silence.

"I'm saying I like you," he burst out, ruffling his hair out of its originally styled look. "I *really* like you. *A lot.* I couldn't even say why… but I wanted to ask you if I could talk to your father…about getting to know you."

"*What for?*" she asked, obtusely. At that point, Elizza was just in denial. *Is he saying…?*

"To *ask* for you," he bit out, almost in annoyance. "For marriage." Then he gazed at her, apparently finished with his speech. His eyes roved over her face, as if trying to absorb the emotions she had trapped inside through the only outlet he might be able to see them. She grew cold, and willed her voice and heart to remain calm.

"I only wish," she said carefully, after pausing to make sure she was master of her emotions, "that I could say it was mutual." Tarseen got eerily still then. He stared at the ground, his hands still trapped in his pockets—remained that way for a few moments. When he finally looked up, he looked a little sad. He pulled his hands out of his pockets and leaned his back against the wall, folding his arms across his chest to regard her carefully before speaking.

"So I take it you didn't like me back then?" he said. His voice was quiet.

Elizza almost laughed. "Do you *really* even like me? From the way you said it, it doesn't seem like it." His eyes didn't waver from her face.

"Enough to put myself in this situation," he said, his voice somewhat clipped. *Self-defense mode switched on*, Elizza thought. "I probably should have just tried to flatter you…"

"Or at least keep insults out of it," she spat back. "Not being able to think of a kind way to phrase it probably should have been a sign it was a bad idea."

"How did I insult you?"

"I'm too outspoken? Remember that? My family is a 'train wreck?' Is that why you told your friend Jana wasn't good enough for him?" He seemed to freeze for a second, absorbing what she said, before wiping his hand over his face in a gesture of mental exhaustion.

"You really want the truth?" Tarseen asked, staring more toward the floor than at her. "Well, it's this: your family could be more respectable. If I didn't really respect and admire you, I would have stayed far away from this situation myself, to be honest. I did avoid it for a while, for that reason..."

"Really? How so? Do you know anything even remotely bad about any person in my family?" Elizza glared.

"No," he admitted. "It's nothing particular. But your youngest sisters run wild, holler at guys on Twitter like they're fishing, your mother is clearly on the warpath to get you all married off to rich guys by any means necessary, practicing Muslim optional. My aunt said she heard that your mom said she wouldn't mind if you guys married non-Muslim men—"

"Oh, your *aunt* told you that?" Elizza interrupted, rolling her eyes. Reliable source if she ever saw one.

"But anyway," he continued, undeterred, his expression cold. "Your dad doesn't even try to keep your sisters out of trouble, and they sure seem to be headed that way. They have 'available' written all over them." At that point, Elizza heard enough.

"My family? What about yours? Your Gaddafi connections, for God's sake? Profiting off of your close connection with a dictator? Or you personally cheating George Wi'am out of property promised to him by your dad?" He looked at her incredulously, his face no longer cold and detached. Now he just looked angry.

"George?" He said the name with unmitigated distaste. "You need to get your stories straight before you start lobbing accusations at people," he continued, after a pause. "That's my dead father you're insulting." Elizza grew quiet. "And I was saving BenAli from himself," he added, as an afterthought.

That was a spark to her scorched earth. "You talk about how my family isn't respectable enough for you, and yet you're the one who lured me into this dark and isolated room. Tell me this: if you really had good intentions, why didn't you talk to my father first?" His face darkened. "We lack respectability as a family, so you think nothing of disrespecting me as a person by approaching me in this *un-Islamic* way?"

"I don't know. Would you think it was disrespectful if it was someone you wanted to ask for you who lured you in here? Let's picture your reaction to George Wi'am in a similar, hypothetical situation."

"You know," Elizza responded furiously—the last straw on the camel's back had finally broken it. "Good thing you didn't ask my father directly. Why embarrass us both by involving my family?" His already red face turned a shade redder. He opened his mouth to speak, and then stopped, instead rubbing the bridge of his nose. After an interminable pause, he seemed to gather himself and recall the time and place of this awkward encounter.

"Sorry to have bothered you, *sister*," he said shortly, before turning his back and walking out of the room. His gait was strange. Elizza couldn't read his predominant emotion from it. Anger? Pride? For God's sake, heartbreak? She stood watching him through the open door as he escaped down the hall, staring dumbly for a half minute before being startled by nearby footsteps and remembering why she was there. He had forgotten the *darbooka* in the end. But maybe he'd just hidden the one they had in the first place?

Chapter Eighteen

Elizza headed for the ladies' side of the banquet hall at first, but halted right in front of the closed door. She couldn't go back in there just yet. She turned around and almost ran down the hall until she reached the lobby of the hotel, where she forced herself to slow down until she reached the outside.

The air smelled of rain, that mix between wet dog and worms ready to spend a rare moment above ground. The atmosphere was heavy with the unshed moisture. She unlocked the door of Shayla's car and grabbed her purse out of the back seat where she'd left it, needing to get her hotel key. Maybe she could go back there to collect her bearings for a few short minutes—reteach herself how to breathe normally. When she emerged from the car, a gust of wind ruffled the loose ends of her hijab into her face, so that when she cleared her vision she was not forewarned of the man's form that was cutting off the light from the nearby streetlamp. She startled and emitted half a scream before her eyes adjusted to the face of Tarseen, and she straightened to a slightly less defensive pose. She stood frozen, stupidly staring at him until he spoke. But that did not happen until he took his hands out of his pockets and crossed and uncrossed his arms at least twice.

"Look," he said, at a loss for what to say. What more *could* he say? His face was all appeal, sort of forlorn but also angry and proud. He put his hands in his pocket as he contemplated the ground, clenching his jaw as he thought about what to say. Finally, he looked up. "I..." he faltered. Stared at the ground for a long moment before changing his mind, mumbling a quick, "Sorry, never mind," before turning around and walking away. She thought she heard him mutter, "I'll send it in an email."

Thunder rent the sky. Elizza's mascara ran down her face in what she was sure would be streams of black as the rain accumulated. She hadn't thought to use waterproof—having expected to laugh rather than cry at this particular wedding. She couldn't go back to the wedding now. She knew she looked a fright. She just hoped she put in enough of an appearance of having a good time to satisfy her friend.

She tried to concentrate on her fear of the lightning and thunder, the coldness of her skin as she got more drenched every second and the water penetrated her clothes and was whipped into an icy frenzy by the wind on this cold early spring evening. Even those less than pleasant sensations were better than contemplating the ache in her heart, and the fury that made it race so fast that she couldn't tell if its pace was due to it or her aerobic exercise as she raced as fast as her high heels would allow toward her hotel room back in the building. She just hoped she was able to get there unnoticed.

***

Elizza was exhausted as she sat in her seat on her return flight home. She regretted booking her flight the very morning after the wedding. She said her goodbyes at the wedding breakfast and caught an Uber to the airport. She had to run to the terminal to catch their last calls for seating. Her reasoning when she booked it was to spend the least amount of time here as possible. Plus she really had a lot of work left on her business plan. She had been staying with Shayla at Kamaal's house. With Shayla off to the hotel with her new groom for a few days, Elizza couldn't really stay there any longer, which is why she booked a room for the night at the five star hotel the wedding was held at, despite Shayla's protests that she was welcome to stay with them for a few days after the wedding. How awkward would that be? Staying at the house of the cousin that previously asked for her, a witness to the first few days of their marital bliss. And now she knew with Tarseen's aunt—and guess who was staying with her?— for a neighbor. No, she'd made a more fortuitous decision than she'd realized.

She tried to sleep during the flight, but couldn't shut off her brain. She had fallen into a dreamless, exhausted sleep when she returned to the house the night before. She was expecting that her thoughts would overwhelm her, but for once, her physical exhaustion took over. Unfortunately, that left her with enough restless energy during the flight to think about all of the things that had happened the day before.

She would never in the world have expected Tarseen to want to marry her, of all people. He always seemed to dislike her—or at least, heartily disapprove of her. She barely cared before, but now she didn't know how to classify her feelings. Except she did recognize rage. That she felt in abundance. She felt rage for all of the insults she had to deal with—for having her family be judged so harshly by someone with an interfering witch for an aunt, for him having torn her sister apart from a good man who might have made her happy, for cavalierly and unapologetically destroying another young man's life just because he was too greedy to part with what for him must be a paltry sum of money. It was infuriating. He was so arrogant he thought she should be flattered by his attention.

But it made her recall all of their interactions in a different light. He insulted her at Linda's wedding…right? Didn't he say he wasn't interested in getting to know her? Or did his words somehow get distorted in her memory? She couldn't remember.

At the college when he tried to answer her question. At the hotel when he forcibly took over the maintenance of her car. His assessment of her business plan, and those meetings. She thought their interactions would have given him even more of a dislike of her than he had reason to have the first moment he saw her. Instead, he decided he liked her and wanted to *marry* her? She wondered why. What made him like her *that* much? She couldn't help being curious.

There were some odd feelings running through her chest. It was hard *not* to be flattered that someone like him, whose high standards for himself she just now got a full look at, found something to like about her. But what a way to tell her about it! And what awful things to say about her family! And…what an unapologetic cad overall. In his own eyes, he could do no wrong. What would it to be like to be married to such a nitpicky full-of-himself jerk? She could only imagine.

But then she remembered the scene itself, and then, the change in Tarseen's expression from when he first spoke to her the day before to when he walked away was what occupied her mind. She was not prepared for any of it, so she didn't give it much consideration at the time. But he started the conversation with such a look of adoration and admiration, she almost flushed to remember it now. His face lit up when she entered the room, but his expression was also tinged with anxiety and something like anticipation.

And the look on his face right before he walked away—a disappointment that almost bordered on grief. Some shade of embarrassment. A hint of a monumental blow to his confidence. And the blow to hers—a look of such surreal disillusionment, as if a veil had been ripped from his vision and he was just now fully seeing her for the first time.

***

Elizza's frugality had led her to buying a return flight with a layover rather than spend an extra $100 for one direct—and the flight that was taking her home was delayed. She was in a real mood. Everything was going wrong. She had one day left of being productive and couldn't even work on anything as she waited. Her mind would not stop to focus. At least, not on anything that wasn't *him*.

She wasn't going to get her business plan done on time—she had to accept that. Her youngest sisters never listened to her. Jana was existing in a fog of depression and was useless to talk to about anything right now. Life, in short, was going spectacularly.

And when life throws you lemons, it says, *oh, sorry, not enough for you yet? Here's a few more.* Her phone pinged an email notification. She glanced at the sender, and then did a double take. She hesitated for a millisecond—she knew she couldn't expect an email from *him* to help her feel better—but she was so overwhelmingly curious she compulsively clicked it open.

From: Firas Tarseen <f.tarseen@SmartConstruction.ly>
To: Elizza BenTaleb <bentaleb.3@midwestuni.edu>
Date: March 25, 2019
Subject: Yesterday

Assalaamu alaikum,

Look… I'm sorry that I didn't write you poetry to tell you that I was interested in getting to know you. I figured I would try to give you a comprehensive look at the ideas that were running through my head as I tried to decide whether to go for it or not. I guess you didn't appreciate what I had to say, and for that, I am sorry. I am also sorry about "luring you into a dark and isolated room." In hindsight, it was a shady thing to do and I didn't mean to disrespect you. My only justification is, I wanted to ask you first before approaching your family. I didn't want family pressure to influence your decision, whatever it was. But now that I think about it, I am surprised I thought anyone could make you do anything you didn't want to do... Your determination is one of the things that I admire about you.

Don't worry—I'm not emailing you to bring any of that up again. I got it—the answer is no, and I already feel stupid for asking in the first place. I do want to address some of the awful things you seem to believe about me, though. That I basically stole George Wi'am's inheritance and that I ended your sister's potential relationship with my friend. Oh, and that me and my family were Gaddafi cronies.

When a guy wants to ask for a girl, the first step is usually to make sure the family is respectable. Most people I know have done that, and that is the way that my family has generally approached marriage. You are, after all, marrying into a complete family. Your kids will interact with the other family members' kids on a regular basis, so it is a necessary part of the Islamic marriage process. Maybe you do things differently in your family or in this community, I don't know. But that is where some of the things that I said about your family came from. I did not mean to insult anyone—I was showing you the struggles I went through to come to the decision that I did, and how my opinion of you led me to overcome all of those things.

I don't know what to say about BenAli and your sister. He has been down this road before, so it is not surprising that he changed his mind at the last minute. I will admit, I did say something to him about not leading girls on unnecessarily, but I wasn't trying to force him away from your sister. From what I have seen, she is a nice girl. When he asked me my opinion about your family in general, I told him what I mentioned to you. Obviously my opinion would be the same—probably stronger in the case of giving advice to a friend. In my own case, other feelings got in the way...

I can't really apologize for that. I would do it again. I was only giving my best advice to a friend, as we are obligated to do in Islam.

If he really cared for her to the degree that she deserves, he wouldn't have abandoned her just because of the things that I said. What her feelings were or are, I really do not know, but I thought either way she would be better off—married to BenAli or left alone to get to know someone else with clearer intentions.

Now to address George Wi'am. His story is trickier. It is hard to type all of this out. It brings back some dark memories I would rather not revisit, but I can't let what you said go. Just to be clear, I am not mad at you and I do not hold anything you said against you. You had no idea about any of this stuff and I don't see you as the type to be naturally suspicious of people. I am sure he made me out to be some sort of criminal, with some added details thrown in because that's what guys do when they talk to women they find attractive. Let me return the favor. Except, what I am going to write is 100% true. I am going to do what I rarely ever do, and say *Wallahi*, in the name of Allah, it's true. I could point you to others to verify this stuff, but I hope you can think well enough of me to accept my oath. I also have to ask you to keep this to yourself. Telling you this is an *amaana* that I know deep down you will not break. So here goes.

George and I have a lot of history. We grew up alongside each other because our fathers were best friends. We started out really close to each other, but after going through the teenage years we both knew we were going different directions. He was wild and reckless and I didn't want to waste my time on that stuff – I knew my father wanted me to learn business so I had something to focus on to keep me out of trouble. George wasn't interested in any of that at the time.

Anyway, his father and my father passed away within months of each other, Allah *yarhamhum*. My dad would have wanted me to support George in that situation, and planned to do so before he died. I offered George to pay his school for him, but he wanted outright cash instead. I told him I did not have that much liquid— okay I lied, but I didn't think giving him that much cash was a good idea. I thought he would waste it all on random things and it wouldn't help his future. I wanted to honor my father by at least helping him somewhat in that area, even if to do it I had to protect him from himself. George did not want that at all, so I told him I could put some property in his name that my dad owned in the US, and he could do whatever he wanted with it. He said okay and wasted no time going to the US to see what could be done about the property – cash it out, I guess. He was young and stupid, and it was in the aftermath of the 2008 housing crisis. He couldn't sell it. He asked me to buy it off of him, and I gave him an offer he didn't like, and on condition that he use the money for school, too. He was not happy that I put a condition on my offer. Anyway, he ended up taking a mortgage out on it, forging my name as the co-signer, and then taking the cash and not making the payments like he should have. It was a stupid move and the bank tried suing me for the money, even though it was their fault they didn't verify my signature or ask for my ID. So, in short, he got the property and he could have rented it out or done something constructive with it, but he chose to steal money from a bank instead. We didn't have the best of relationships before that and this basically ended it. I didn't hear from him for a few years after that.

Then, two years ago, I get a call from my aunt in Libya. My sister lives there with my aunt because I want her to have some stability and family, and I can't really provide that for her because of the business. That's another reason I've been thinking seriously about marriage lately– I want my sister to have a woman to get close to and help her out in life.

Anyway, my aunt found her computer open and read some messages exchanged between my sister and George. He was trying to convince her to run away with him to America. I have no idea what his game was and I really don't care. Maybe they did love each other, but at that point I was not going to let my sister tie herself to a person like that. I suspect he was just using her to mess with me, but who knows. I still have this anger about it, so I try to avoid him whenever I can. Of all the places to find him, I didn't think I'd run into him in the town where I took a university appointment, but I guess life is funny like that sometimes.

So that is my explanation for everything. Hopefully this explains my intentions. Whether you accept them or think I made good decisions, this is the unadulterated truth about what happened.

Again, I'm sorry if what I said offended you or if any of this bothers you. But I had to get this off of my chest, just so you know.

I wish you well with everything you do. I don't know if we will ever see each other again, so please accept my well wishes for your future. I hope you go through with your business and take my suggestions as constructive criticism, as they were meant to be. And I hope you find happiness, Elizza, whatever that looks like for you.

Take care of yourself,

Firas Tarseen
SmartLy Constructed, Inc.

P.S. oh, my family never did business with Gaddafi. Dunno what else to say about that, except... it never happened and I have no idea where that rumor started. Probably George again...

***

Elizza put down her phone. She should try to sleep on the flight home. She needed sleep. She couldn't sleep. Thoughts whirled around incoherently in her mind, and it was a while before they settled.

She could not think clearly enough to determine whether or not Tarseen had absolved himself of all the charges she'd lobbed at him. She was more concerned with what his revelations revealed to her about herself. She'd jumped to some extremely clumsy assumptions. She remembered accusing him of being part of a family of Gaddafi supporters and flushed. Only the fiercest anger could have allowed that half-baked rumor to escape her lips. She couldn't really remember half of the awful things she said to him. It was all a blur of heat and fury. She could only remember feeling the adrenaline rushing through her body with a passion that had as much to do with being alone with a physically attractive male as it did with her being furious. Her anger, discomfort, environment all conspired to release the usual tact that held her tongue off from uttering the truly unutterable. And thus the filter between her brain and mouth was temporarily disabled. She did not know what she thought and what she believed anymore—it was too soon and too raw for her to even begin to disassemble that scene and all that followed. But she was pretty sure that she could not bear to face Tarseen again, his flattering admiration of her notwithstanding. Or, perhaps, mostly because of it.

Chapter Nineteen

www.google.com

Kawthar typing...

What does "sketch" mean

Then:

Sketch in a sentence

~

Hey Elizza. Can I borrow a hundred dollars?" Leedya said, breaking the distracted silence in the car, having volunteered to pick her up from the airport. Now Elizza knew why. She was just pulling into their driveway, her left hand halfway out the open window, enjoying the frigid but fresh early spring air.

"Are you kidding? I can't believe you even need to borrow money from me. Don't you get paid for those video promos you do?"

"Yeah, some of them. Look, I'll pay you back."

"I'm not worried about that. You can have it. On one condition, though." Leedya inhaled warily.

"What's that?"

"You listen to my business tutorial. I mean, you're running a business. Time to get serious. You can probably write off half of your closet using it for business purposes."

"Well, I get some of it for free."

"Okay, but then you buy more stuff and use it in your videos with the money you get, right? So, that probably accounts for what, like, half of what you make?"

"More than half," Leedya said, looking at her nails. "More like minus." She flashed a winning smile.

"I shouldn't really be encouraging this," Elizza said thoughtlessly. Leedya bristled.

"Uhh, why not?" Elizza looked at her sister's expression, her face falling.

"I didn't mean… it's just… murky. What you're doing." She winced. She was too tired for this conversation.

"In what way? I started a business, for God's sake. You're the one who always tells us how the best thing we could do for ourselves is have our own businesses!"

"Yes," she responded. "I do. It's just what you're doing in particular. Teaching girls how to wear makeup and look attractive—as they wear a scarf that's supposed to mitigate their attractiveness. It's sort of an oxymoron." Leedya rolled her eyes.

"You're unbelievable," she said finally.

"Leedya, don't get offended. I'm not trying to discourage you. I just want you to be more reflective about your actions instead of just blindly falling into things. Even think about taking the money you've generated from this and investing in something else later."

"Basically, you want me to think like you."

"I want you to think about serious things, like why we are Muslim, what the purpose of life is, what you want your future to look like, how you'd like to see the world change…"

"Yeah, so you want me to be like you." Elizza ignored her.

"You're basically teaching other girls the wrong way to wear hijab, the blind leading the blind."

"I *am* reflective, Elizza. I'm teaching girls who might struggle with hijab a way to wear it and not hate it and actually find it fun and fashionable."

"You can still accomplish that and do it within the parameters of what's right."

"Okay, what's right then? And how do you know you're doing it?"

"Do research. Look in the Qur'an and *sunnah*. There's not much variation of opinion about the big things."

"Except there are like, 1000 different ways women practice wearing hijab." Elizza sighed.

"I'm not telling you what to do," she finally said. "I'm just saying you should ask yourself that question before you do things. About anything you do in life. Am I doing the right thing?"

"Islam doesn't have to be that complicated," Leedya retorted hotly.

"Islam isn't a passive religion, either. You have to get up and pray, withdraw money to pay *zakah*, be kind to people, fast during Ramadan. It colors our whole lives. We should be asking ourselves before we do anything whether it's pleasing to Allah or not."

"I could have gotten this lecture from Maryam," she muttered.

"I'll help you either way, Leedya," Elizza said. "I'm just saying, try to grow up a little, think about the future."

"You know what? I'll get the 100 somewhere else," Leedya said before exiting the car and slamming the driver's side door.

***

"She's right, you know," Maryam said from the doorway to the house. Leedya turned around, livid that self-righteous Maryam overheard their conversation.

"Yeah, wouldn't we all love to be like you and do *dhikr* of Allah twenty-four seven and cover from head to toe all the time and when we get married our birth control method will be *tawakal ala-Allah*, but most of us live in the real world," Leedya huffed.

"I know what I am supposed to do," Maryam said, "and I do it. Unlike you, who could care less, know practically nothing about Islam, and put up a token resistance when you come across any rules you feel restrict you in any way, without really trying or caring to find out what the true answer is." They stared at each other, angry and uncompromising, both equally incapable of understanding or compassion when it came to the other.

***

Elizza ran up the stairs to her room after greeting her parents, and breaking up the tense standoff between her sisters. She found Jana lying down in her bed, staring up at the ceiling of their room. It was a relief to see her sweet face, but Elizza couldn't help but worry—Jana did not look happy. She needed someone to talk to, however, and after pausing to think for a second, decided the distraction might prove helpful to Jana, and wasted no time breaking into her story. Jana was all sympathy and concern. She could see through Elizza's hilarious recounting of the events and was worried about her sister.

"Okay," Jana said thoughtfully when Elizza was finished. "We're fixating too much on the negative. Tell me something good, Elizza."

"Ugh Jana, I can't right now. None of your forced positivity training today, please."

"Oh, come on Elizza, just try. Can't you think of anything? Or this, tell me something good about the proposal."

Silence.p

"Anything at all. Come on it's not that hard. The guy has some good, material qualities at least," Jana tried, hinting hard.

"Here's one: if I would have said yes, I'd have been spared the drama of a mother-in-law." Elizza burst out laughing at Jana's stricken face.

"Oh, don't look at me like that. I already felt bad for the thought as soon as I said it."

"*Allah yarhamha,*" Jana said, dampeningly.

"*Allah yarhamha,*" Elizza dutifully repeated.

"I was getting at, you know, that he's rich," Jana said.

"Oh, is he? I hadn't heard. I mean, no one *ever* mentions it," Elizza said.

"Or that he's handsome." An image of intense black eyes, ruffled curls, loose tie circling a strong neck, came unbidden into Elizza's mind.

"Money isn't everything," she said, ignoring Jana's second comment. "It can turn into a way your husband tries to control you." Jana sighed.

"Elizza, don't take this the wrong way, but sometimes I think you could turn any smile into a frown." Elizza couldn't help taking it the wrong way, and stayed silent. She thought of the past few months of tiptoeing around Jana's disappointment, hinting at depression without being able to come out with the words, willing her to get help but unable to hurt her so. *Likewise,* she wanted to say. But didn't.

Chapter Twenty

ThatRiverInHeaven posted.

My baby sister's 18th today. She's officially an adult! Just want to say how amazing I think you are, Leedya. I love you so much and feel so privileged to be your sister. You're beautiful, strong, smart, sophisticated, tasteful, and a truly wonderful person. Happy Biiirttthdaaayyy!!!!

🎈 🎂 🍰 🎁 🎈

LeedyaMinLeebya posted a reply.

Aww, thanks babe. 🖤

~

Time passed slowly after the excitement of the wedding. Elizza's concern for her sisters Leedya and Jana grew. Jana came home everyday from working at the daycare and fled directly to their shared room. She would answer Elizza politely if she asked any personal questions, how are you holding up, did he even promise you anything, etc. but wore such a pained expression each time that she eventually gave up asking.

"I think it's *ain*," she heard her mother whisper to her father in the hallway outside of their bedroom door. "She has been depressed for months. It could even be *sehr*."

Leedya was another story. She would only exchange the barest of words with Elizza. Yes. No. Fine. Sure. She roped Kawthar into giving her the cold shoulder, too, albeit with an apologetic expression on her face every time she had to cut Elizza's attempts at conversation short. So Elizza tried to steamroll her hurt emotions by putting all of her effort into her business plan.

***

"Kawthar, what the hell?" Leedya shouted from the hallway some days later. Elizza rolled her eyes at her laptop. She needed to go to a coffee shop or something. It was impossible to get work done at home sometimes. "You're so nosy!" Leedya spat, storming past the doorway of Elizza's room clutching a journal. "My personal thoughts are *none* of your business! Mama!" Kawthar ran after her sister.

"But who is—" Kawthar began. Leedya cut her off, grabbing her arm and changing directions, pulling Kawthar along with her. "Go to our room," she ordered through clenched teeth. "We'll talk there. Just let me call off Mama."

Elizza sighed, closing her laptop and packing supplies into her book bag. She had to leave if her sisters were planning a sisterly chat for the afternoon; she wouldn't be able to concentrate with their relentless murmuring vibrating the thin wall between their rooms. Opening her drawer for some more pens, she came across her own journal, sitting undisturbed from its position from last month when she'd written in it. She picked it up and ruffled through the pages, still stiff, like a book no one was interested in reading.

"I'm sort of offended no one's trying to read mine," she said aloud.

"That's because everyone knows nothing interesting is happening in your life," Leedya chimed in, popping her head in for the second it took her to lob the irresistible insult. Elizza groaned. *I bet the events of these last few weeks would make for some interesting entries.*

***

"Leedya's 18 today," Kawthar said, unnecessarily. They had all been peppered with reminders from Leedya herself—not to mention from the five different social media accounts she was signed up with—that her birthday was coming up. "We're all officially adults now."

"God save us all," was Maryam's response.

"Adulthood is a mindset," Elizza rejoined, looking pointedly at Kawthar.

"My gosh, how did we all get so old?" Jana chimed in despondently.

"We are *not* old," Elizza said. Why couldn't Jana just move past her depression, for God's sake? *That* was what was getting old. "Okay," Elizza said, changing the subject. She finished her coffee and stood up. "Quickly, before she comes down, who's going to pick up the cake?" No one volunteered. "Kawthar? The book store is literally right next to a bakery."

"I don't have any spare money," she whined. Elizza rolled her eyes and handed her a $20 bill from her purse.

"It's a *luxury* bakery, Elizza. It's going to cost me more than $20 to get one." Elizza sighed.

"Never mind," she said, grabbing her money back before Kawthar could stuff it into her purse. "I'll get one from Dairy Queen. She gets off at, what, 6?" Kawthar nodded. "Okay, will you all be here?"

"Birthdays are *haram*, Elizza," Maryam said. "We shouldn't copy the *kuffar*."

"Don't sing the song then," Kawthar said.

"Just have some cake with us," Elizza added. This came up every time someone had a birthday. She would object for form's sake—to save her own soul from the sin of celebrating something that was not specifically allowed by the Prophet Muhammad (PBUH) as an allowable celebration—but she had a sweet tooth and couldn't resist a good piece of cake. Elizza herself was not big on birthdays—they seemed a pointless celebration, celebrating a person not for an accomplishment but for their serendipity of being born on a certain date. And she was unsure and unclear about the *sharia* aspects of whether or not it was really permissible, or just disliked. But their parents started the tradition when they were little, and she hated to discontinue it now. Her parents barely cared anymore, but how exactly was it supposed to end? Which sister got to blow out the very last birthday cake with the family assembled all together? Ending a tradition like that was just too political for her to even want to attempt—better to just keep plowing forward. If their mother had her way, they would all be married off soon anyway and then they would all be living their own lives and it wouldn't come up anymore.

"Jana?"

"I'll be home," Jana replied. *I know,* Elizza wanted to say. But didn't. She rarely went out after coming home from the daycare.

"Will you make sure Mama doesn't go out?"

"Sure."

"So, what are we getting her?" Kawthar asked. Jana and Elizza shared a look.

"Nothing?" Elizza replied.

"Oh, come on! She's turning 18."

"I'm sure that's exciting. For her," Elizza said as she walked out the door. Kawthar could go spend the money she didn't have on a gift from them all, if she liked.

***

6:25 p.m. It took Leedya about 18 minutes to get home from the community college, before she'd blast through the front door like a hurricane, leaving a trail of her stuff from the doorway to her room like little fashionable breadcrumbs. You never had to guess whether or not Leedya was home. But she wasn't home yet.

The sisters sat waiting, gathering around the table with the cake at the center, 18 candles stuck messily and unevenly into the cake in random spots (Kawthar was decidedly *not* a perfectionist), waiting to be lit. Their mom and dad asked to be told when Leedya actually got there, each too busy with their own pursuits to want to hang around waiting—their own pursuits being 1) gossiping and 2) trolling news about Libya on Twitter and Facebook, respectively.

6:35 p.m. Elizza lost patience. *Where is that girl?* she wondered. *She's way past traffic jam late now.* The ice cream in the cake was starting to glisten.

"Kawthar, call her." Kawthar obliged. They all listened as the sound of Leedya's phone ringing played into the silence, and Leedya finally picked up.

"Hey, where are you?" Kawthar demanded, then paused. "What? You didn't tell me about that," she said accusingly. "She didn't invite me?" Her face darkened as she listened to Leedya's reply. "Okay, thanks for nothing." She abruptly hung up, grabbing a giftwrapped present out of her pocket and tossing it onto the table.

"She's not coming. She's spending the night at Maariyah's house." She walked out of the room, throwing out, "one of you guys can have that," gesturing to the gift before the kitchen door slammed behind her.

Odd, Elizza thought. Leedya didn't mention it earlier. She walked to her mother's room to share the news.

"You told her it's okay?" she asked. She loved Shayla to pieces, but her sister Maariyah was a bit wild.

"Oh, she asked me last night," Umm ul'Banaat replied, rubbing her tired eyes. "*Insait*, I was half asleep." Elizza walked downstairs, back into the kitchen, and was greeted by a sad sight. An empty dining table, chairs all askew from being carelessly vacated by the sisters, the cake still sitting on the table, melting so much that there was a trail of ice cream dripping onto the floor.

***

Elizza was uneasy. She couldn't help wondering what her sister was up to. The "sleepover" seemed too abrupt to be the real story. She was nostalgic for the little girl she remembered growing up—stubborn and willful but with an affectionate charm that meant you were unable to stay mad, and an innocent beauty that made you feel like a monster if you ever tried to discipline her.

Just to torture herself, she picked up the digital picture frame sitting on Leedya's desk, swiping through the pictures and focusing on the ones of Leedya. Leedya smiling as a toddler, eating a piece of corn. Holding Leedya's chubby form in her arms, her face showing the strain of holding her sister up as Jana frantically tried to take the picture before Elizza dropped her. Their mother and all of the girls in front of the lions at the zoo, Leedya in pride of place at the center. What she wouldn't give right now to go back to those simpler moments in her family's history.

The next morning, Elizza woke up later than usual, having spent a sleepless night waiting for her phone to ping with news about Leedya from Shayla. Jana popped in, a reassuring smile on her face.

"I heard you tossing and turning. She's fine, Elizza. She just got here a few minutes ago. She's taking a shower."

Elizza exhaled in relief. Grabbing a robe, she went to Leedya's room and sat on her bed, feeling affectionate and momentous, like maybe she could come to some understanding with Leedya that would bond them forever, and her voice could be the voice of conscience in her head when her dumb friends tried to tempt her into doing things she knew were wrong. She felt like her mom.

Her eyes lit on Leedya's phone, tossed carelessly on her bed before going to the shower. The screen was lit up and open on a message from Maariyah.

Last night was a blast. Fancy running into him again, lol

Elizza's heart sank. She didn't know what the message meant, or who it referred to, but it showed a deceitfulness about her little sister that she did not want to acknowledge, and that worried her.

Leedya walked in, a towel wrapped around her midsection, hair damp and curling.

"Elizza, what the hell?" she screamed, grabbing her phone out of Elizza's hands.

"What did you guys get up to last night?" she asked, trying to keep her voice nonchalant. "We were told you'd be spending the night at Maariyah's house."

"We did sleep there eventually," she said. Elizza just looked at her. "What, are you going to yell at me now? Slap me with some Muslim guilt? You'll want to fetch Maryam for that."

"I just want to know where you were," Elizza said.

"We didn't go anywhere bad. Just went to a coffee shop. It's not a big deal."

"But if it's not a big deal, why did you feel like you had to lie about it? I mean, obviously there was a 'he' involved." Leedya glared.

"Yeah, when you go out places, there will always be 'hes' involved. That's how the world works. I'm not just going to stay home all the time to avoid being around guys. I do my due diligence by wearing hijab, so…" Elizza sighed. She was getting nowhere. She didn't know what to do, but she was wasting her time now. She needed to think it through a little more. But by herself. Jana was in no state to help. She had her own issues to be sad about. Kawthar…was Kawthar. Maryam was too self-righteous to give good advice about things like this. Her mom would probably be unconcerned. Her dad… she couldn't even imagine trying to tell her dad Leedya lied to them. As much as she loved him, he had a naivety about his daughters that she pathetically and probably wrongly wanted to protect. He was light and carefree and unconcerned, and she wanted him to stay that way. She could shoulder the burden of this problem. What was one more thing to worry about? She was pretty sure she was capable of it, she just had to think. After she made up some sleep.

CHAPTER TWENTY-ONE

Abu l'Banaat posted on his wall: I am not going to post who I support politically in this mess. Quite frankly, both sides are wrong, and Muslims should not be fighting each other. The only thing this war will accomplish is pushing Libya further away from the healing it needs. May Allah (SWT) stop the fighting.

LibyaMlitiaMan replied to Abu l'Banaat's post: Gaddafi supporter.

Hiftar4Libya replied to Abu l'Banaat's post: Militia sympathizer.

~

The second half of the semester passed gently and uneventfully. She did not have to worry about running into Tarseen because, like BenAli, his appointment only spanned half of the semester. By some miracle, she was finished with all of her graduation requirements, and on time, too. *Finally.* She walked through her favorite part of the university, a memorial grove that cut through the center of the buildings that housed the different colleges, feeling light at heart and oddly free, the feeling stemming from the moment she dropped her 50-page plan into the drop box of her advisor's office for the last time (he was old school and still insisted on printed copies of everything). But a little dismal too—she didn't know what to do with her time now. She supposed she should start taking practical steps to start a business—and apply for jobs in the meantime. But she shut her thoughts down. She didn't need to worry about any of that now. She just finished the most stressful semester of her entire school career. She needed a break from all of the *worrying.* And the planning. She just needed to relax, and enjoy the accomplishment.

So it was a shame that at that moment, she had to run into Leedya walking through the grove, accompanied only by George Wi'am. Elizza almost groaned aloud. *I don't need this.*

She gave Leedya her signature look of disapproval. George tried to catch her eye with a smile, but she refused to smile back. At her coldness, he looked to the younger sister and said a quick "see you later" before making his escape. When he was out of view, she turned to Leedya.

"What are you doing?" she asked, her voice disappointed. "I've talked to you about walking around campus with guys. It's not a really Islamic thing to do. We have to try to keep our distance from men we aren't related to."

"You do it," Leedya spat back.

"What? I never—"

"George told me you were walking with Tarseen one night," she said accusingly. Elizza fumed. Of course he did. What a scumbag.

"I wasn't—I didn't walk with him because I *wanted to*—" she tried, but Leedya just smiled.

"Looks the same from far away. You have to be more careful about your reputation, Elizza." She tsked. Elizza opened her mouth to retort, but then gave up. There was a difference, she knew. She *thought*. But she was so befuddled and angry and worried about seeing them together she couldn't summon the words. And Leedya's self possession and quick jabs sometimes left her speechless.

***

Elizza graduated with the minimum amount of fanfare. At her graduation ceremony, she had her father and Jana there to support her in the crowd. Her mother was still angry at her for Shayla stealing Kamaal away. Her two youngest sisters made excuses not to go, and Maryam said she had a headache.

Her party was also a rather dismal affair. She didn't really want a party, but her father didn't want the momentous occasion of his daughter earning her MBA to pass without some sort of celebration. At Elizza's insistence, they kept the guest list short, only inviting the very closest of her parents' friends. And there wasn't any excitement to the party—Fathiyah was living with the reality of having married off a daughter who now lived far away, and the other mothers were rather sad that two bachelors came and left their small community and were able to escape with their bachelorhoods intact. Her sisters mostly all didn't want to be there, or around the Libyan community—and it showed. The guests left early, there were way too many leftovers for their family to be able to finish before it went bad (even after the guests were sent home with as much food as could be pushed on them), and Elizza was scarcely richer than she had been before the party—she had a $225 credit after the expenses of the party were deducted from the cash gifts she received from her guests. Her mother was the manager of their family's food budget, and insisted on it, reminding her repetitively that her father's salary could not be extended to pay for the food for all the parties they seemed to have to throw for her every other year.

***

There was one thing that Elizza could still be excited about. She had her trip to Libya to plan. Whether she would still be able to go in the end was touch and go—the political situation, and fight over Tripoli, worried her father, and he insisted that she wait to book her trip for a few weeks to make sure that the Mitiga Airport would still be operational—and safe for civilian travel. In the end, her father heard that Shayla's parents were going to Libya for one of Shayla's younger aunts' weddings, and Elizza's father asked them if she could travel with them. Of course they graciously said okay, and so Elizza's trip was booked. She was only going to stay for two weeks instead of the month she was counting on for that summer, but she would take what she could get.

It was fun planning a trip to Libya. She had to do loads of shopping to make sure she had a gift each for her cousins and other relatives in Libya. She had outfits to plan, and some suitable dresses for weddings to find, because there would invariably be several weddings to attend, the month of June being the start of the Libyan wedding season, the political instability notwithstanding. Libyan men still wanted to get married, and Libyan brides would still want their full three to seven days of festivities, and the associated marital gifts to boot. In fact, she was already invited to attend the wedding with Shayla's mother.

And after contacting her uncle, and going into more detail than she expected him to ask for about her business ideas for Libya, he asked her to bring some pamphlets from the suppliers she already found, and some figures on the funding. Easy enough. She had that already compiled in a binder for when she had to submit them for the final review she had where three professors from the Business College asked her assessing questions about her business plan. Thanks to Tarseen, she had been well prepared for what would have otherwise been an overwhelming and intimidating barrage of skeptical interrogatories.

Her uncle offered to help her with whatever she needed. So, her hiatus on not thinking about her future, which never really started to begin with, ended, but she was excited to be able to use her trip to further her own personal goals. She would stop worrying about marriage and men and family problems—no, she really would this time! She would focus instead on making her dreams a reality.

***

Several more weeks went by, and it was time to be off. She bid her farewells to her parents once her luggage was collected by the door, the one dismal suitcase her flight ticket allowed, and a small carry-on that held all of the stuff she really cared about—her cash, phone, some real gold jewelry to wear to parties, and business plan materials. Shayla's parents rejected Abu l'Banaat's offer to drive them to the airport—their daughter Maariyah was staying behind because she had to work and would drop them all off.

"And she doesn't want to miss the conference with Leedya," Kawthar added angrily.

"What?" Elizza asked. She hadn't heard anything about a conference. But then she heard the sound of a car honking out front and had to make her way out.

She hugged her mother goodbye. Her mother stood there limply for a second before giving in and enfolding her daughter in her arms, almost crushing the air out of her lungs.

"*Mitizaleesh minni li'anni saaba maak, anna saaba maak li'muslahtik,*" she said softly. *Don't hold it against me if I am hard on you; I'm only hard on you for your sake.*

"I know," Elizza whispered back.

Aloud, Umm ul'Banaat was up to her usual tricks. "We should take all the girls to Libya. They'd have a better chance of getting married there. At least Jana and Maryam."

"You're probably right," Abu l'Banaat responded. "I'll ask your brother to run an advertisement to see if any Libyan men want green cards."

"Be serious. Elizza could have used some whitening cream before she left, though. Why didn't we have someone send us some for her?"

Leedya was at work, but Elizza hugged Jana, Kawthar and Maryam goodbye as well, none of whom had any desire to go with her. She hugged her father last.

"Promise me you won't get married when you're there," he said, and she laughed, but when he didn't join in she started to think he might not be joking.

***

Shayla's parents were checking in to the airport the old-fashioned way, at the desk. She had a few seconds to make a phone call. She dialed her father's number.

"No, I didn't forget anything," she said hastily, when he answered. "What was Kawthar saying about Leedya going to a conference?"

"*Shinu?*" he asked, infuriatingly slow. "You need to talk to Kawthar?"

"*No*, Baba," she said, trying to keep her voice level, glancing at Shayla's family now approaching the check-in desk. "Kawthar said Leedya is going out of town with Maariyah…." She paused to let him catch up.

"*Aih*," he said finally. "She asked us to go listen to Islamic lectures with her friend. It sounds like a good thing for her to do. She and Maariyah are going with a Libyan friend of mine from college and his family." Elizza's heart sank.

"It's dangerous, Baba," she said. "Don't let her go. Just because the family is Libyan doesn't mean they're going to do a good job watching out for her."

"It's going to be fine, insha'Allah" her father replied. "He's an old friend of mine, he'll watch her like his own daughter. It's a Muslim convention, *aslan*."

Hasn't Baba ever heard of the Islamic convention acronym T-shirt's? she wondered.

Islamic Society for American Youth: I'm single are you?

Then again, no, he probably hadn't. He hadn't been out from under his rock in ages.

She sighed loudly.

"She'll be fine *habibti*. Don't worry. Just make *duaa* for her if you're so worried."

"Make *duaa*. Okay, make *duaa*. But you're *also* supposed to tie your camel to the tree after your *duaa*, Baba!"

He burst into merry laughter. "You want me to tie your sister up, is that it?"

"Really, Baba? Now of all times you miss the real meaning behind a metaphor?" But she had to go. Shayla's parents were almost at the front of the security line and she had to hang up. That was that then.

She couldn't get it off of her mind. Her worry continued to spiral through her all throughout the security check, the wait for the calls to board, and boarding. At takeoff she had adopted a new mantra to get herself through her worry and her takeoff fright. *Not my problem not my problem not my problem* she repeated. She tried it for several minutes before giving up on relieving either worry. *Who am I kidding? It's always my problem.*

Chapter Twenty-Two

Elizza's arrival to Tripoli, Libya went unexpectedly smoothly. No unexpected delays or missing baggage.

She was extremely happy to see her Uncle Muftah and his wife. Her mother's brother was different from his sister. He was extremely laid back, and with a non-interfering personality. He always made you feel like your judgment could be trusted, only offering to help whenever he felt like it could be of benefit to you. Between all of the social calls Elizza made with his wife and the three weddings she had to attend and catching up with her cousins on both sides of the family, he made it a point to take her around to meet some business contacts and to see some of the more technologically advanced buildings that existed. But, he told her, he was saving the best for last.

"We have a company here that builds smart houses," he said proudly. "I want to take you to their model home. Maybe we can talk to the owner and see if he is willing to invest in your business."

"Wow," she exclaimed, after getting over her initial shock. "Do you even have to ask? Make the appointment!" She was exhilarated. An actual potential investor? Her uncle checked with his wife and was told she could spare Elizza the coming Sunday. They agreed to go early in the morning then, and she thought about what she should wear. The power blazer, she finally decided.

***

The sun beat down on her back. Sick of waiting for her uncle to give up on gaining entrance to the architectural wonder, she roamed the garden through which the entrance road was paved, keeping her uncle in view. It was pure beauty. It must take a special kind of persistence, she thought, to keep the grass so green in this hostile environment. She stopped at the edge to read an informational plaque on the garden's design. Not persistence then, she thought with respect to the architect, just ingenious engineering.

She didn't have the patience to read *all* of the informational plaques in the garden, descriptions of engineering and mechanical wonders that at times went way over her head. But what she did absorb blew her mind. She highly doubted it could all be cost effective. The genius was overwhelming – structures she previously thought were palm trees shifted to shade her as she walked down the main path through the garden, sort of like the ones she heard protected visitors of Masjid Al Nabawi in Medina. She wondered if the architect stole the idea from them. The fountains, she read, were built to replenish their water by absorbing it from the atmosphere, even in this arid environment. Windmills and solar panels were artfully disguised a number of ways so that you had to be looking for them to detect how this garden was fueled – palm trees were windmills, structures you took for centerpieces of abstract art were really just there to hold tiny solar panels in place. Flowers blended seamlessly with the colors of the fruit or vegetable growing nearby. Everything was irrigated with underground hoses that were, she read, installed with motion detectors and hoses that sprayed in two directions so people walking through would also be sprayed with a cool mist on days when the temperature went over 27 degrees Celsius. Today was such a day, and as she traipsed through the garden, she was kept from suffering the heat of the sweltering weather.

It was like a science museum, fun to walk through not just because of its beauty, but because at every turn you beheld a new engineering or mechanical marvel. It was glorious. She turned back to find her uncle, a smile gracing her face as she thought about how much he would love this garden – scratch the house, just seeing this was enough. But her view of her uncle in the distance, presumably still chatting with the guard, was obscured by the figure of Firas Tarseen walking down the path toward her.

Chapter Twenty-Three

I n the several seconds she had before Tarseen would look up and
notice her standing unobtrusively to the side of a palm tree windmill, Elizza contemplated doing several things: ducking behind a
nearby fountain, jumping *into* the fountain and holding her breath until
he walked away, pulling her scarf up to obscure half of her face in a
makeshift *niqab* (a tempting option, but the power blazer/*niqab* combo
might draw *more* attention to her rather than less), book it fast in the
opposite direction, book it fast in *his* direction and hopping into the car
before he could get a good look at her face, driving away if he decided
to come investigate (she'd come back for her uncle later). Unfortunately,
her mind thought of so many possibilities that she couldn't decide on
which option to take before the sight of one end of her hijab rebelliously
blowing out like a flag to one side of her signaled his attention her way,
and he looked up—

If Tarseen was the type of person to do so, he would have emitted an audible gasp. He wasn't, however, so his reaction was confined
to stopping in his tracks for several seconds, blinking for several
more, blushing to an embarrassing degree, and visibly attempting
to collect himself before walking over to where Elizza was standing,
ruffling his hair in a gesture that Elizza by now recognized was one
of confusion and/or nervousness.

Elizza's eyes roved shiftily around her before he looked her
way, but at the sight of his arrested expression, she just stood where
she was, resignedly, her heart beating so hard she could feel it in
her throat, caught like a deer in headlights, the redness of her face
warring with the redness of Tarseen's. But after watching him for a
few seconds, she oddly felt herself becoming more at ease, drawing
strength from his nervousness. It's not like she was *trying* to bump

into him, she reasoned. She was as surprised to see him there as he probably was to see her.

"*Assalaamu alaikum*," he said, his voice soft, but also guarded.

"*Walaikum assalaam*," she responded. Neither spoke for a few seconds, just bumped their shifty gazes, each trying to watch the other's face without being caught doing it.

"What are you—" she said finally, at the same time that Tarseen said,

"How did you—" They stopped. Tarseen finally finished his question when she steadfastly refused to go on.

"How did you hear about us?" he said finally. Like a new business asking a customer that question so they knew how to apportion their advertising money. Elizza stared for a second, confused.

"My uncle brought me here to see this new smart house," she said. "I'm sorry, are you...? Is this your...?" Tarseen nodded in understanding.

"I see. So, you didn't know... your uncle didn't tell you that I own it? But of course not. Why would he?"

"I don't think he knows we know each other," she responded. *Obviously.* He nodded again. He was doing a lot of nodding. It seemed to have turned into another gesture he was leaning on to hide his nervousness. He then either forgot to avoid her gaze, or stopped trying to not get caught watching her, and let his gaze consider her. With that, Elizza felt the full force of her own nervousness, confusion and embarrassment return with a vengeance. She had to stop herself from wringing her hands just to have something to do with them.

"And how are you doing?" he asked, softly again. "And your family," he added, as an afterthought.

"Good Alhamdulillah. Just... visiting Libya." *At the same time as you*, she thought. *Odd, that.* "Doing business research, too," she added ruefully. But she also had a challenging gleam in her eye.

"Great, great," he said abstractedly. His mind was clearly elsewhere. The thought made her oddly glum. "Sorry, I don't want to keep you from your uncle. He must be waiting for you—"

"No, he's just trying to … gain entrance to see the house," she finished with an amused half laugh. Tarseen smiled back. His left hand ruffled his beyond mussed curls.

"I think I can help with that." With that, he turned and walked back down the path.

"Abdullah," Tarseen called to his security guard. "It's okay. I'll take them around." Her uncle turned around in surprise. Elizza face grew impossibly more heated. He'd be accompanying them the whole time? She wasn't sure she could maintain her composure for that long. The two men exchanged *salaams*, and Tarseen explained his acquaintance with the family. He then led the way to the front of the house, and opened the door to allow them inside.

Tarseen showed off his work, explaining the technical features of the house and the decisions the company came to about the specific materials to use for certain things. Wood floors were in vogue in Libya at the moment so they preserved the style without actually using wood, which would be hard to upkeep in a sandy environment, by using tile painted to look like wood. He had a hard time keeping his eyes off of Elizza, so much so that it drew her uncle's notice, and that drew Tarseen's notice, and his face turned a shade of red to rival Elizza's—after which, he avoided looking at her at all, except to gauge her approval whenever he talked about the technical aspects of the house, convincing himself he was keeping his expression neutral and inquisitive, as open to suggestions from Elizza as he would be to any other guest taking a tour of the smart house.

Elizza's uncle took it all in with interest. He couldn't wait to tell his wife.

***

There was an odd serendipity to them meeting here, by chance, at this time and this place. Elizza trailed her uncle and Tarseen, her nerves on edge, watching the pair avidly, noticing everything. Tarseen ramping up his charm to the max. Paying attention to her uncle's movements and allowing him to linger as long as he wanted to in any particular room. His gaze resting on her when her uncle was busy inspecting some technical feature for a few minutes. But he seemed so embarrassed every time she noticed that she came to realize it was happening involuntarily. Her last remaining objection to him—as a *person*, she told herself—was his lack of courtesy. And yet, the way he was treating her uncle—all solicitousness and consideration. Kindness and interest, asking him for suggestions on improvements and what price points would be affordable for everyday Libyans. Slowing down when her uncle seemed to need rest. Rummaging his cupboards for soda to offer them, even though it was obvious he was not overfamiliar with where the refreshments were kept.

It was remarkable how much he had changed. Like he'd showered in a waterfall of humility. It was a good look on him, Elizza had to concede.

But it didn't change the fact that she came from an "unsuitable family," she tried to remind herself. Whether or not he was being nice now, it didn't mean he'd ever want to interact with her family beyond this chance meeting.

"Brother," Tarseen was saying, "I wanted to ask you a favor." Her uncle was agreeing to anything before he even finished his request.

"Would you come to my house for dinner tomorrow? My sister really wants to meet your niece. Are the rest of your family here?" he asked, turning to Elizza. "It would be nice to have you all as guests."

Her uncle couldn't assure him they'd be there fast enough.

"It's just me with my aunt and uncle," Elizza said, when her uncle had gotten the logistical details. She searched his face for relief. He either felt none, or was really good at hiding his feelings. She was not sure which.

***

She stood in front of the car after running the AC on max and closing the door to let the cool air circulate. Tarseen was talking to her uncle, making sure he had all of the details for tomorrow's dinner invite and siphoning some details about what they planned to do for the rest of their stay—at least, that's how it seemed to Elizza, or did she just want it to seem that way? *Do I?*

She narrowed her gaze on Tarseen. Really looked at him, while he was preoccupied with her uncle. Wavy brown hair. Tanned forearms. Athletic build. Tall. Quizzical eyes. Could seem judgmental at times. But that had regarded her with kindness on multiple occasions. Handsome even, she was surprised to be able to admit to herself. He met her gaze then, catching her mid-assessment, shooting her a brief, questioning look before she turned away.

***

Droplets of water from the fountain peppered his tanned face and crystalized strands of his gleaming, shiny dark brown hair. He stood in front of the fountain, dress pants impeccable and held up by a stylish matching belt. His top half, however, revealed his nerves, the neck of his baby blue shirt loosened to reveal the indent between his collar bone, his sleeves rolled up clumsily to reveal muscled forearms, a concession to the heat, a light speckle of hair.

He stepped toward her, his black eyes caressing her face, drinking in every detail.

He paced back and forth, his fingers loosening the medium length locks of his hair, formerly styled in place. Then he stopped, stared, spoke, his voice shaky with emotion.

"I just—can't help it," he bit out. "I ...still love you." Elizza was frozen in shock.

And then she woke with a start, her heart gurgling in her mouth. She smoothed back her hair, trying to induce calm. It was just a dream. Then she remembered. *God*, she thought. *The dinner. What an inconvenient dream.* And then, *I really need to stop reading romance novels before bed.*

Chapter Twenty-Four

She didn't realize that Tarseen did not actually live in his smart house. But then again, she should have. Of course, he had a place that existed before this.

It was a nerve-wracking dinner—even though she entered the house to be welcomed in by his sister, Jumana. Tarseen was nowhere to be seen—presumably welcoming her uncle from a different entrance to the house that led to the space where the men would sup. When she was led to a large room lined with thick cushions set against the walls in seating customized for the room in the Libyan decorating tradition, she saw Kareema BenAli sitting like a primping bird, her back ramrod straight, her hands delicately clasping a narrow Libyan tea glass and saucer.

Elizza felt antsy and uncomfortable in her own skin, despite the fact that Jumana looked to be about as nervous as she was. She suspected that the cause of her discomfort was not even sitting in the same room with them. Kareema would not allow the satisfaction of throwing her off. She was more like an irritating fly. If she could just get in a good swat, she'd be golden.

Kareema's exuberance towards Jumana was disturbing to watch. It was like watching a person who hated dogs try to gush over the cuteness of a puppy.

"Come sit by me, *habibti*," she said, when Elizza and her aunt sat down after exchanging greetings with their hostess. "Tell your guests about going to the beach with my brother yesterday." At one point, she grabbed Jumana's hand and placed it on her arm. The poor girl's face showed how awkward she felt, but of course she was too polite to pull away. There was a possessiveness about her behavior. When the food arrived, she selected the choicest pieces and placed them in front of Jumana. She poured a beverage and forgot, or purposely omitted, asking the guests what they'd have.

It was hard for Elizza or her aunt to get any words in to Jumana, even though they tried. Elizza tried asking Jumana playfully if she had gotten any marriage proposals, and Kareema cut in.

"Don't be modest," she said. "You probably got more proposals than Elizza and all her sisters combined!" And then she laughed in a way that seemed meant to include Elizza. Elizza did not oblige her by laughing along.

"Tarseen said you're extremely smart and talented, and women like that don't stay unmarried for very long," Jumana said, and then blushed about being so forthcoming. Kareema's face darkened.

Elizza's phone rang then. She was not inclined to answer, wanting to avoid being rude by answering a call when invited to dinner at someone's house, but saw that it was her father calling. From America. It had to be like, 2 a.m. there right now. She answered the call.

"*Assalalaamu'alaikum*," she said, in greeting. "Couldn't sleep, Baba?"

"*Walaikum'assalaam*," her father answered, forgetting to laugh. "Elizza," he began. "I didn't want to disturb you, but…"

"It's never a disturbance to get a call from you, Baba."

"Where are you now?" Elizza couldn't get herself to say "Tarseen's house."

"Eating dinner with friends," she said instead.

"Can you excuse yourself?" he asked.

"Okay…" she agreed nervously. This was bad. She gestured to Kareema and Jumana. "I'll try out in the hall. Bad reception." She got up to walk out of the room, but her aunt held her wrist before she could leave, shoving her hijab and abaya at her to put them back on. Right. She probably shouldn't go out into the hall without her hijab with Tarseen in another room of the house. When she was safely out of hearing, she demanded, "What is it, Baba?"

"Leedya didn't get on the plane from the conference," he said abruptly. "Maariyah and their friend hid from her parents that she wasn't there until end of flight. They haven't seen her since last night."

"What? How could they not notice?"

"I don't know, Elizza."

"What did her friends say? Do they know anything?"

"Leedya told them she would get home separately from them and since she was with a Muslim boy they didn't think it was that bad."

"Muslim boy? Who? Someone we know? Why would a Muslim boy get her into trouble like that?"

"They couldn't—or wouldn't—say at first," her father said heavily. Then he sighed. "But then Kawthar said that she might know who it was. But she isn't sure if they are still together. She seemed to think Leedya disappeared alone."

"Who, Baba?"

"George Wi'am." Elizza's heart dropped. She conjured a mental image of his face, green eyes, friendly smile. Muslim boy? He wasn't a "boy," he was a grown man. It was almost hard to believe. Except when she remembered him telling lies about Tarseen with that same beguiling smile on his face.

"We have to find them," she whispered softly, her eyes filling with tears.

"I know, Elizza. We are talking to Kawthar and Dr. Trabulsi is talking to his daughter. I just wanted to see when you get back. I think it is soon, right?"

"Three days—but I can come sooner!"

"No need. Just make *duaa*." Her father hung up, and Elizza cried. But she couldn't indulge her tears for long—or more like sobs at that point. She heard the creak of a door open and turned away to hastily wipe her eyes with the end of her abaya. She didn't have anything better to use.

"I'm sorry," someone said. A male voice. She looked up into Tarseen's face. "I was just coming for—are you okay?"

"Yes, I'm fine," she said, straightening up and letting her abaya fall to the ground. Tarseen looked dubious, and concerned.

"You know you can trust me?" he said, eyeing her tear-stained face. "Whatever it is…" he almost looked pained to say it. Elizza was having a hard time getting her emotions under control, and at the worst time. She took a deep breath.

She had to get a grip on herself. Kareema would come out to investigate any minute. The last thing she needed was for her to come across her in such a state. No one could know about Leedya. It would destroy her father to get calls from self-proclaimed well-wishers who were really calling to get the latest scoop so they could pass it on to the rest of the Libyan community. She dried her tears and turned to Tarseen.

"Do you need your sister?" she asked.

"I was just going to ask her where she keeps the Arabic coffee. I hear your uncle likes it. But what's wrong?"

Elizza didn't know what to say. Should she tell him? Looking into his dark eyes, though, she felt like she could trust him with anything, and he would be a locked vault.

"My sister is missing," she finally said. He looked at her uncomprehendingly.

"Missing?" he said. "Which one? What do you mean, missing?"

"Leedya, of course," she almost spat. "My dad gave her an inch of freedom and she took a mile." Tears leaked from her eyes again as she thought of alternative scenarios. "Either that or something awful has happened…" she trailed off, turning away again to wipe her eyes with the sleeve of her abaya.

"*Insha'Allah* everything will be okay," he said finally. He looked uncomfortable.

"What do you mean she'll be fine?" she asked, knowing as she spoke that she was taking out her feelings on an innocent bystander. "Haven't you ever seen the movie *Taken*? She's a beautiful 18-year-old girl who took advantage of her freedom for the first time in a big city and probably went and did something stupid. The police won't do anything because she's 18 and they probably think she just ran away from her oppressive parents."

"I'm sorry, I didn't mean to downplay your worry…"

"I know. I'm sorry. I didn't mean to snap…" He shook his head. "It's okay, Elizza. You want me to go get your uncle?"

"Yes, please." And with that, he left the hall. Elizza watched him walk away, and had the odd sense that some source of light was leaving her life.

***

Her uncle didn't agree with her father. He approached the situation with urgency, buying Elizza enough calling cards to set her up to make hours of phone calls if she had to change her flight to an earlier one. She had an earlier return flight within hours, with hardly a spare minute to say goodbye to everyone she needed to. Her uncle dropped her off at the airport and offered her a quick hug, asking to be kept updated on the Leedya situation. And with that, she was on her way back to America. She stared out of the airplane as it ascended to greater heights in the sky, watching the cement brick houses of the Libyan natives and their sandy land speckled with rare spots of greenery get smaller and smaller, the literal distance growing at 400 miles an hour, taking her farther and farther away from the country that held at least a part of her heart.

Chapter Twenty- Five

@RandomLeebeeyyah: @LeedyaminLeebya you haven't posted anything in like, a week now. What gives? And who am I supposed to go to for hijabi fashion advice now?

~

Eliza's entire body felt stiff, including her mind. It felt like an old clock that hadn't been oiled. Each thought was a painstaking grind of gears that did not want to move. Still, it was good to be home. Here she could indulge in the illusion that she was doing useful things. She could pat Kawthar's back, hand Jana some tissues, redirect Maryam's "I told you so" tirades, make her mother some *talbina* "for the depression," and probably, most importantly, keep hold of her father's cell phone for him. He really didn't need to see all the missed calls or hear the smug voicemails of distant acquaintances who were calling out of "concern" and wanted to know the minute something was recovered about his "poor daughter."

Every once in a while, she'd roam Leedya's shared room with her sisters, telling herself she was looking for some clue. But really just making herself miserable, wondering if the third inhabitant of this room, and the owner of this bed and all those clothes in the closet would ever make it back to reunite with them all.

***

The alarm sounded. Elizza turned it off, fighting her exhaustion. 3:00 AM. The last third of the night. That magical time that Allah (SWT) promises to answer all prayers. Elizza was sorely in need of some extra guidance in her life. She felt like it had been ages since she'd slowed down and prayed *tahajjud*. She felt the need to reconnect with Allah, to reach out to Him and ask for His guidance. Her life felt so fast-paced that she'd forgotten to slow down and take time to thank and worship her Creator to the best of her ability. Maybe this test was—Allah's way of gently pulling her back to Him.

Elizza didn't really know what she was asking for. She washed her hands and mouth, nose and face, planning her *duaa*, but just feeling overall miserable. What was the purpose of this test in her life? She washed her hands, rubbed her wet hands over hair and ears and over her socks. She hastily donned a prayer skirt and scarf and started her prayer. In her prostration, she asked for forgiveness. She asked for guidance. She asked for ease. She asked for Leedya to come back, to become better, to trust them. Then stopped, struggling with how to word her request to Allah, to complain to Him about her struggles.

"Please, oh Allah," she eventually whispered onto her prayer rug with her forehead and nose touching its soft strands, "help our family feel more at peace and find our way successfully out of this test, and You know best." And then added, "and please, oh Allah, help me find my way out of mine. Ameen."

***

"How could she soil herself like that?" Maryam asked the next day, outraged. "How could she soil *us* like that?"

"Maryam—" Elizza tried.

"We all saw which way she was going and dragging Kawthar along with her. I told Mama a million times she needed to make her cancel her Instagram page. We all knew it would lead to nothing but trouble."

"Are you done?"

"Isn't she afraid of getting an STD? She has no idea what this George Wi'am has been exposed to."

"And we have no actual proof she's been exposed to him, so to speak, and shouldn't talk that way."

"Oh, come on!"

"Regardless of what we might assume. It's actually wrong to assume the worst. Anyway," she cut off Maryam's urge to argue *fiqh* with her, "how is any of this helping?"

"She had it all planned out," Maryam snapped.

"How do you even know?" Elizza asked.

"Didn't you see the email she sent Kawthar? Baba made her print it out. It's on his desk."

Elizza turned around without answering to go find the paper, thankful that her father was not in his office. She read the following email:

From: LeedyaminLeebya@gmail.com
To: thatriverinheaven@gmail.com
Subject: Sorry

Hey Kawthar,

I'm sorry to put this all on you, and double sorry I didn't tell you about any of this. I know I usually always keep you in the loop, but I was just feeling so restricted and had to get away. Everyone is so stuffy, and everything is always haram and I just couldn't take it anymore. I had to just break away. Anyway I'm fine so everyone can just chill. Me and George are going to live together and get married when he can afford to support us. He isn't getting far with Uber but he's applying to go back to school and to get scholarships so he should be able to soon. And really we'll be fine with what I bring in as long as I stop buying stupid stuff with all of it, as Elizza advised. Anyway miss you all and it's fine just tell everyone stop freaking out already I'll be married soon and hopefully after that Baba can live through the scandal of it all. It will be a relief to everyone anyway. You'll all be better off for a while without

Your Sai3a Little Sister
Leedya

***

Elizza knocked on the door to her little sisters' room and opened it. Kawthar sat in front of one of the windows in their room, open to let the cool summer breeze flow through, staring glumly at the moon.

"So what's going on with you, Kawthar?" she asked. "How are you holding up?"

"Fine," she said shortly. Elizza just stayed silent. "Baba's never letting me go anywhere after this."

"Because he sees you as Leedya's shadow," Elizza replied bluntly.

"I'm not her shadow! I'm my own person! I would never have done something so stupid."

"I'm not sure Baba knows who you are yet."

"So it's my problem he hasn't tried to get to know his daughters better?" Elizza tried to hold onto her patience.

"No," she said. "I'm saying, take your future into your own hands and show him that you, unlike Leedya, are capable of being responsible when given a little bit of freedom." No answer. She changed tacks. "Have you heard from her since that last email?"

"No." Pause. "I never answered." There was a world of hurt and embarrassment in that reply. Elizza got up and kissed her sister's cheek, surprised to catch her lips on a tear.

"Goodnight, Kawthar," she murmured, her heart breaking for her little sister. My hardest trials and tests in life thus far, she thought, are watching the people that I love in pain.

CHAPTER TWENTY-SIX

T arseen stood outside of the hookah bar, hating what he decided he had to do, what he gave himself the responsibility of doing. He blinked hard at the tacky fluorescent lights of the sign, taking a deep breath as he scanned the faces in the room.

He found him sitting with a relatively small group of friends near the only fireplace the lounge could boast of, inhaling and exhaling fumes, in deep thought, as his friends regaled themselves with funny stories from a recent youth. He caught George's eye. Slowly putting away his pipe, George excused himself from his friends before donning a smug smile and following Tarseen to another table.

***

He wished she could see him at this moment. No, scratch that. He wished she could see into his heart at this moment. There was always something uplifting about doing a good deed—purifying, almost. He felt clean and light, like the blackness that accumulated in his heart from all the pent-up hate and rage had been erased; erased, though, as from a computer. Erased for all practical purposes, but still recoverable by an astute computer programmer or hacker intent on digging up the dirt. He still hated the guy, but the feeling was a sort of distant antipathy no longer seared into his heart, like your dislike for a certain food, or hating to hear nails scratching on a chalkboard. Hatred no longer consumed him.

And anyway, there was no longer any room in his heart for hate. Not when it was so overcome, buoyed even, by this overwhelming love.

CHAPTER TWENTY-SEVEN

They all waited with bated breath as their father listened carefully. When the person on the other end went silent, he took a deep breath.

"*Bah, barak Allah feek ya* Syed. *Inshoofook,*" he said, and they said their *salaams* and hung up. They stared at their father, waiting for him to speak.

"Well, they found her," he said. "They did their *kitab*, so *alhamdulillah* for that. They have an apartment and he is planning on going to school. He got some sort of scholarship." Her father went silent. Everything he said was astonishingly good. But his expression and manner were both deeply sad. The sisters hugged each other in relief and disappeared to their rooms, except for Elizza, who enfolded her father in a hug.

"She will be okay, Baba," she said. "She made her own decision in this, so it's out of your hands now. She can take care of herself."

***

"*Alhamdulillah,*" their mother said, a smile lighting up her formerly drawn face when her daughters burst into her room to give her the news. "Who would have thought Leedya would be the first to get married?" she asked happily.

"We'll do a wedding party here," she stated firmly.

"No," their father said with uncharacteristic vehemence, walking in behind his daughters.

"She's married. She needs a wedding."

"She doesn't deserve a wedding," he yelled. "She ran away from us all, caused us a lot of worry, shamed our whole family. I am not inviting anyone to celebrate on her behalf when she didn't show us any consideration."

"Baba," Jana tried.

"No," he said again. "I should have seen this coming," he added, giving Elizza a meaningful look before leaving the room.

"We all knew something like this would happen," Maryam said redundantly. "She was getting worse and worse. She was like water rushing toward the zenith of a waterfall." She paused so her family could appreciate the artfulness of her metaphor. The room was unusually silent. Leedya would never have let her finish a speech so long. "She was living with that guy for how long before they actually got married? No one will say. Her marriage doesn't change what she did. And now you all just want to invite her back like nothing happened? Like we're all okay with it. She won't learn anything." Silence.

"Or am I wrong?"

"We're just grateful nothing worse happened to her," Elizza finally said.

"If we don't forget the scandal, no one else will," their mother said practically.

Chapter Twenty-Eight

LeedyaMinLeebya updated her relationship status to Married.

LeedyaMinLeebya updated her status. Yep, you read that right! No, I didn't click the wrong button. I'm MARRRIEEEDDD!!!!! 💁

So, gentlemen, you can all stop sliding into my DMs with your marriage proposals. I'm taken.

You know who you are.

~

L eedya had been gone a total of six days. She was due to come home later that afternoon, and Elizza wondered how she would be received by the rest of her family—particularly their father.

Just what did parents do when their kids came back home after crossing the line of appropriate behavior their families set for them? How did parents handle it when their son was brought home by the police for shoplifting, or their daughter came home, apologetic, saying she totaled the new car her parents just bought for her—and rear ended someone's Lexus to boot. What did other parents do when their kids got suspended for missing too much school, when for all their parents knew they were top students in their high schools?

Their parents did not have too much disciplining to do of their five daughters, mostly because the two oldest were good at keeping the others in check and disinclined to get up to any real mischief themselves. The only one who ever gave them any real, consistent trouble was Leedya herself, but her type of mischief was mostly financial, spending too much money and having to get her sisters, or in the rare case her sisters could not or would not pay the balance of her bank overdraft, her parents, to bail her out of a financial hole. The other type was accidentally using foul language in front of her parents and staying out later than she had permission to. Those occasions were usually dealt with by their father by enforcing some sort of period of house arrest. He would, either to amuse himself or as a tactical form of punishment, order her to assist Maryam with whatever chores she had to complete for the week. By doing that, he was also able to save himself the bother of lecturing her.

But this was an entirely different scenario. And now, Leedya was officially folded into someone else's sphere of responsibility. This was going to be interesting.

***

Elizza opened the door to a pair of green eyes she would formerly have described as beguiling—and did do so, actually, in her journal—but that now reminded her of a snake's, conniving and malicious.

"You think I'll make it out of here alive?" he asked in lieu of a greeting. Charming smile. Well, Elizza thought, stepping aside to let him in, her sister and George had that in common at least. He stepped inside and Leedya jumped out from behind him to engulf her sister in a surprisingly tight hug. Elizza just hugged back for a moment before murmuring quietly, "We missed you, Leedya. We were so worried." That seemed to break the spell. Leedya hopped away again and pasted on her version of the charming smile—just as dazzling and just as fake.

"I was never in any danger, you guys. And as you can see, I am fine! And married! I've achieved Mama's goal for my life at age 18, before all of you. I bet Mama is so proud."

***

Coffee runs were for getting away. Paying twice the price you reasonably should have to pay for a cup of coffee was worth the money when the objective was escaping the toxic energy that is sometimes emitted from those that love you the most. A run was sorely needed now. The problem was, Elizza could not conjure a conversational blade sharp enough to cut through the silence between her and Leedya in that car. Every subject seemed taboo, and Leedya was clearly leaving the trouble of finding a subject to her.

"Are you happy?" she finally ground out, then winced. Hardly a neutral subject. Leedya turned on her signature sunny smile. The one she used to deflect attention.

"What girl wouldn't be happy with those gorgeous green eyes staring down at her day." Elizza rolled her eyes. She *would* go there.

"So, what happened, Leedya?" Elizza said, breaking the silence that had fallen again.

"It's not as bad as everyone is making out. We always planned to get married, it's just that he didn't have the money or resources to get married at the time."

"But you guys went behind everyone's backs."

"We love each other! Baba wouldn't have even considered anyone who couldn't support me. We were just trying to get him to allow us to get engaged."

"You guys didn't even try, Leedya. That's pretty much the one difference between honorable men and dishonorable men. Honorable men have the courage to approach your father when they want to marry you. The other type are content to lead you on for years, expecting and taking everything and giving nothing in return, refusing to offer a firmer commitment and always making excuses about why they can't marry you."

"That's my husband you're calling dishonorable."

"We will all love him for your sake, Leedya. I didn't mean to insult him at all. But I wanted to point that out, so you don't sell yourself short or fail to value yourself. Valuing yourself as a person, demanding your rights and respect is just as important after marriage as it is before marriage." Leedya said nothing, just looked out the window of the car.

"So you guys will be all right? Have enough to live on?" Elizza tried again.

"Yes," Leedya said shortly. "I'm sure you heard about the scholarship."

"Yes, that's really amazing," Elizza replied. "He found out about that right on time, didn't he? So it pays living expenses, too?"

"You don't have to sound so skeptical." Elizza glanced at her quizzically.

"I wasn't—"

"I hate it when people know about things and then act like they don't to see what you say." Leedya glared at her. "Mama does that all the time. It drives me nuts."

Elizza tried not to let her face show how confused she was. "I just thought that if it's that good a scholarship we should tell our friends about it," she tried again.

Leedya snapped. "You know there's no scholarship!" she yelled. Elizza had enough. She pulled over abruptly, the liquid in the coffee cups sloshing loudly.

"So how are you guys going to support yourselves?" she asked, trying to let her genuine concern show.

"*Tarseen* set up a trust," she finally answered. "To pay his school and living expenses until he finishes."

***

Elizza fled to her room as soon as she returned home. She couldn't get more information out of Leedya. Now at least she knew that Tarseen was somehow involved in getting Leedya out of the mess she crawled herself into, but she didn't know why. *What did it mean?* She dug her journal out of her desk drawer and flopped onto the floor, her back against a wall. Maybe she could puzzle it out if she wrote about it. But as she hastily flipped through the pages to find a blank one, she landed across a cringe worthy former entry from the night of Linda's wedding, blushing as she read the words "emerald eyes", "tanned face," and "warm inside" as she skimmed the page. She blushed furiously as she tore it out of her journal.

It was weird having your sister marry a guy you once thought you had a crush on. One moment, you're wondering if that significant glance shot your way was fraught with hidden messages for you, and the next, you're realizing you were never the object to begin with. It was a humbling revelation, in the end. But Elizza didn't regret the fact that George chose differently. She only regretted that she ever harbored any gentler feelings toward him at all—and wrote embarrassing entries about him in her journal. Which she must remember to rip out and destroy. She flipped through the pages to commence immediately—this was not a thing she could afford to forget.

"Whatchya doin'?" Leedya asked, blowing a bubble of gum and smashing it with her lips as she stood in the doorway, watching as Elizza clumsily crumbled the pages she'd found so far into balls and turned her back on her sister from her spot on the floor, trying to nonchalantly find a place to stuff them. *Of course Leedya of all people would walk in on me doing this.* How obvious would it be to cram them under the bed? she wondered.

"Just some...bad poetry," Elizza mumbled, resorting to covering the pages with a blanket. "Iambic pentameter is way off..."

"Or hiding some interesting journal pages?" Leedya stated calmly, bursting a figurative bubble this time. Elizza stood up then, throwing her journal onto her bed and turning around to cross her arms and engage in a staring contest with her littlest sister. There were still some things it took age to master, Elizza thought with bluster.

"My life isn't quite as boring as you all think," she answered, a small smile touching her face. Leedya just looked at her, unwavering, and thoughtfully smacked her gum.

"I already saw your sad George entries," she said, to Elizza's chagrin. "Frankly, they were really boring."

"Wow. For someone always raising hell about everyone else being nosy..."

"I mean, it's totally understandable," she went on, undeterred as usual. "Anyone would be taken in by his lovely green eyes. But come on, Elizza, your entries lacked any feeling whatsoever. If you really had a crush on him, you probably could have come up with better adjectives than 'emerald' and 'sea glass.'" Elizza just stood there. Well, what could she say? At least she could skip a Google search of "where do you take paper when you want it incinerated" and just toss the stupid pages in the trash like a failed writer now. She had no idea where she would have found a place to burn them anyway. Leedya smiled sweetly before turning around to go. But had one more parting shot to take before leaving the room.

"If I were you, I'd take a closer look at those steamy Tarseen entries. Seems to be something brewing there."

***

Things settled down quickly, to Elizza's surprise. It was amazing how quickly they had all adapted to the situation. The gossip about Leedya flared upon her return home with rampant speculation and constant inquiries--and then died down again. People's calls to congratulate the family on Leedya's marriage, masking a desire to siphon out every single juicy detail of the story, peaked the third day Leedya returned home and by the following Saturday, they did not have a single phone call about it. It was a sort of progress.

George was decidedly *not* living with them, and Leedya had still not been given official permission to go off to live in wedded bliss with the man who was, for technical religious purposes, her husband. Their father decided to treat their *kitab* as a sort of "engagement" period, despite the fact that the entire community knew that she had run off, and stayed out several nights, with the guy. But all of the girls, Leedya included, sidestepped the issue with their father. He was not ready to relinquish her so easily or so quickly. Leedya roamed the house in a sort of purgatory, not knowing what was going to happen with her marriage but unwilling to face her father alone to challenge his prohibition that she go off and live with him right away. To Elizza, however, when Leedya roped her into a reconnaissance mission, her father merely said, "I'll know she is actually ready to be a married woman when she comes into my office to talk to me about it herself." Elizza agreed, so she kept his statement to herself. Leedya, though, was convinced her father was out to get her and doing everything he could to sabotage her marriage.

"If I wanted to leave and go live with him right now, no one would be able to stop me," she said mutinously. "I'm only staying here to humor him." That's what she said, but just where he was living, she would not say outright. They all listened to her rants dubiously until Elizza finally had it from Kawthar that his "stipend" for school was not going to be given to him until the start of the semester in a month. And that he was sleeping on friends' couches until he could afford the deposit on an apartment. Elizza wondered what Tarseen was up to making him wait so long to get an apartment, and sort of wondered if he did that to give her father some time to digest Leedya's abrupt change of marital status.

For Elizza, the more she thought about what Tarseen did, and everything she had learned about the man that he is, the more depressed she became, a level of depression to rival Jana's, except instead of solitude and quiet, she manifested hers through moodiness and impatience with her family. What is wrong with me? Elizza often wondered. She should feel happy. Her sister was not human trafficked after all. That was a good thing. That was a great thing. And yet…

But she actually knew what was wrong with her. She couldn't stop thinking about Tarseen. He was on her mind constantly. Her brain was flooded with memories of him—his sheepish smile, his muscular forearms, his face flushed passionately has he tried to control his anger when they argued. And now his enemy was her brother-in-law. She didn't know what that meant, exactly. How much she'd have to interact with the fellow, how often she'd have to see him throughout her life. But she was pretty certain that George Wi'am's future aligning up with hers, however slightly, took her future away from aligning with Tarseen's, and she was somewhat surprised that the thought was leaving her feeling heartbroken.

Elizza thought her first love would be an uplifting thing. Fluttery and warm, a pathway to thoughts that would bring a becoming flush to her cheeks and heat her from the inside out, no matter the external weather. The realization of this love was scalding, searing. Her organs felt like they would melt with embarrassment. She felt like a burgeoning pubescent girl all over again—awkward in her skin, moody for no reason—or for too many reasons to get a grip on, to really comprehend. She felt like all those people who bought pizzas with their bitcoins a week before the stock skyrocketed astronomically. She didn't realize…and was it really her fault she didn't? She was stupid and judgmental, but did he have to be so secretive about everything? So private and forbidding? So mysterious? Her mind drifted to his physical sum. But she stopped herself. In that direction lay madness.

Elizza wished that things were different. She wished the thing with Leedya had never happened. If Tarseen was concerned about her family's respectability before, now it was impossibly tarnished. She had a sister who had been practically living with her boyfriend.

Why did Leedya have to go wild at the precise moment she became aware of the state of her heart?

But the issue was deeper than the one with Leedya. If she was trying to wish for something useful, she'd wish that Leedya's ache for superficial joy would stop making her so restless, that she could find a source of lasting joy in her life that would bring her peace. She wished Jana would find the love of her life that she yearned for. She wished Maryam would be less rigid and find some way to relate to other humans. She wished Kawthar would learn to find out who she really was, and not waste her inner light mirroring others. As for herself, she was so overwhelmed by the rest of her family's issues, she couldn't even bear to think about it.

***

Umm ul'Banaat came running into the hall. Elizza hadn't seen her mother run for several years now—there must be some exciting things afoot.

"*Habibi*, I just spoke to Fathiyah," she said breathlessly. She paused for a few minutes as her husband and daughters allowed her to catch her breath, nibbling at the remnants on their plates from breakfast. Umm ul'Banaat had left it to take a call from Shayla's mother.

"I just had it from her—Just who do you think is coming back to town for a second teaching appointment?" There were some groans at the table as they all anticipated Umm ul'Banaat's answer.

"Mohamed BenAli!" she cried. "And that moody friend he takes everywhere with him," she added as an afterthought.

Elizza's heart thudded loudly in her chest as she got up to put her dish in the sink and slink quietly into her room.

Shut up, she told it sternly.

CHAPTER TWENTY-NINE

"Jana, go open the door," their father said as he stood up to fold his prayer rug, having just finished praying *dhuhr* with Elizza and Jana. Elizza would have thought her father above scheming on behalf of his daughters, but she revised her opinion when she accompanied Jana to the door and it opened to reveal BenAli and Tarseen. Jana, having thrown a prayer outfit (a floral skirt held together with a plastic waistband and a waist length matching floral hijab, both dingy from daily use) over the pajamas she was wearing to pray in, flushed in embarrassment, backing away from the door to clear a way to the hall. Elizza, scarcely less shocked and embarrassed, at least had the presence of mind to invite them in. And to have put on actual clothes earlier that morning—she couldn't stay in pajamas past noon.

"You're here to see my father?" she asked, and when they both nodded, pointed to the halfway open door to the right of the hall, unable to look either man in the face. Her father met them in the doorway and shot Elizza an amused smile. Elizza's look in return was decidedly not. She turned to Jana and all but dragged her shocked sister up the stairs, slamming the door behind them as they reached their room, ready to ponder what it might mean.

"Nothing," Jana was certain. "After all this time, they came to see Baba. That's all." Elizza just ignored her, opening their closet to scan it for something presentable for Jana to wear. It was better to get dressed for battle, just in case.

***

Elizza dragged Jana down to the kitchen to wait out the men's visit. Maryam, Leedya and their mother were already assembled at the table, not wanting to miss the excitement. Leedya called Kawthar at the bookstore and convinced her to get permission to leave work early – it wasn't everyday your sister might be getting engaged. Kawthar burst into the kitchen a few seconds after Elizza and Jana.

"Did I miss it?" she asked breathlessly. Jana flushed furiously, glaring at them all.

"You're all making this so much harder than it has to be," she said.

"Give yourself some credit," Leedya said scornfully "He wouldn't be callous enough to show his face here again if he wasn't here for that purpose." Jana looked thoughtful. "The question is, do *you* want him after all of that?" They all turned their glances towards Jana, wondering too. She was silent.

"Of course she does," Umm ul'Banaat answered.

"Is he a good Muslim?" Maryam asked. Leedya and Kawthar groaned. "No, seriously. That's the one thing I haven't heard anyone discuss yet. Does he pray? Go to *jumaa*?"

"You saw him at *jumaa*, Maryam," Elizza reminded her.

"Pay *zakah*? Fast during Ramadan?"

"Tarseen does all of that, and he probably wouldn't keep a friend that close to him if he didn't, too," Elizza said without thinking. Her sisters gaped. "I mean… I'm assuming…I think," she finished lamely. "Baba will ask about him."

The kitchen door opened suddenly, and their father walked into the kitchen.

"Well, Jana," he said. "BenAli is sitting in my office, waiting to talk to you about something." He regarded her carefully, watching her shrink into herself at the statement. "You don't have to go in there," he added. "I can tell him to go away."

"And never come back!" Leedya added dramatically, but then ruined it by chuckling. Elizza regarded Jana, too. She was withdrawn, thinking carefully. Probably contemplating her future. Her wants. Her emotions. Elizza didn't think she really understood until this moment the depth of Jana's feelings. How heartbreaking it must have been to become attached to a person, put your hopes in the validity of his intentions, to really think that he wanted you, and then to become convinced later down the line that it all must have been in your head. And then, after convincing herself that it must be because she was worthless, not that great of a catch, to have that same person come crawling back and doing the thing they all anticipated he would do much earlier, only several months later. With no hint or forewarning whatsoever. If it were her, Elizza thought, she would be demanding answers.

Jana shook herself after a few moments. Her family gracefully, and surprisingly, allowed her the time she needed to collect her emotions. She looked up with the fiercest expression any of them had ever seen on her face, a look of determination, some fury, some pride, all of it wrapped in a cocoon of hidden passion.

"I'll go," Jana said finally. She walked out of the room with her shoulders back, her head held high, and fiery red hi lo shirt swishing out behind her as she walked through the door.

***

Elizza left the kitchen too, wondering what happened to BenAli's friend, telling herself she wasn't wandering the house hoping to run into him. She was in luck—because she didn't. Sighing, she walked down the hall to creep upstairs to her bedroom, but stopped just outside of her father's office door when she heard BenAli's earnest murmur.

"I'm sorry, Jana," he said fervently. "I don't know what to say for myself. I thought I wanted to get married. I was seriously looking for a partner in life, and then I stumbled upon you. And you were—are—perfect. I was so excited, and so sure about you…. But then it all hit me at once. The burden, the weight of what getting married truly means. How you don't just marry a person…you marry into a family. And how that person, that woman, puts her trust wholly and completely in you. How I would be responsible for another person, and potentially an entire family not long after that. It was all too real, and I started to panic. I recently just lost my father, the backbone of our family, and it was a crushing experience to realize that the person you relied on was now gone, and you had to figure out your life on your own. I realized just how much my father was to me, meant to me and really supported me. And then I imagined someone placing that amount of trust on me, and I wasn't sure I was ready for that yet." BenAli's speech was greeted with silence. Elizza could not see through the door. But she could only imagine how Jana was feeling.

She felt that she had eavesdropped, unintentionally, long enough, but then BenAli went on. His voice was farther now, as if he had moved around in the room. Deeper into the room. Probably closer to Jana, Elizza thought with a smile.

"But I started going into withdrawal," he said, in a deeper, more solemn voice. "Withdrawal from seeing your smile, hearing your voice. There was something amazing in my life, something to look forward to and to make my life seem brighter and full of hope. And because I was stupid and cowardly, all of a sudden it was all gone. And I realized what was on the other side of the coin. What if you *didn't* rely on me? What if I *didn't* get to support you? And the reality of that was … probably the most depressing thing I could imagine ever *not* happening to me."

And what would—could—Jana say to that? Elizza had invaded their privacy for long enough. She blushed, ashamed of herself. Even her mother hadn't stooped this low. *Oh Allah, please help her make the best decision for herself in this life and the next*, Elizza supplicated silently at the foot of the stairs. Putting it in the hands of Allah was the best *duaa* she could think of, her default. Heart sighing for her sister, she crept upstairs and into their room to sit on her bed, knees wrapped against her chest. She turned to look out the window, the quiet street of the neighborhood. A small red headed boy riding his scooter in front of his blond mother on a bicycle behind him, the late summer breeze gently swaying the mature trees that shaded the street they lived on. She squinted her eyes at the car sitting in the driveway, and blinked when she saw who was sitting in the driver's seat, staring blankly into the steering wheel. Tarseen, with his floppy hair mussed, drooping over his moody eyes. He was so close, a mere 30 feet away at most. But to Elizza, he seemed worlds out of reach, as he looked up to regard her sitting watching him from her window, and then looked hastily, deliberately away.

***

The front door of the house slammed, and Elizza's heart dropped in disappointment (she was secretly rooting for BenAli to prevail—what a speech!) when her fears were put to rest by her mother's loud *zaghroota* echoing through the house. Loud enough for BenAli to hear, for sure, as Elizza watched him look back over his shoulder at the house and smile broadly before almost running to the car to give his friend his good news. Tarseen hopped out of the car to enfold his friend in a congratulatory bear hug, which looked like the kind of hug an older brother would give to his younger brother, a proprietary gesture, like BenAli's happiness was by default a subcategory of his own. Tarseen released his friend and they both got back into the car. Tarseen turned on the car, and turned his head a fraction of the way towards Elizza's bedroom window, perhaps able to see her silhouette in the window before turning back and accelerating out of his parallel parking spot in front of their home, disappearing down the road.

***

BenAli hastily booked the community hall to host a small engagement party for himself and Jana, to follow the *fatihah* to be held at the masjid earlier in the day, technically an Islamic marriage, but that they all agreed to regard as the engagement period until the *walimah*, wedding party, could happen a few months later. BenAli was for holding that party as soon as possible—no matter how much money he had to put forward to get it booked. Umm ul'Banaat smiled at his eagerness. Abu l'Banaat frowned and told him he didn't need to be so hasty. Leedya quipped, when BenAli left, that everyone would assume Jana was pregnant if they did it so fast.

The day of the party arrived. It was attended by all in the community. The mothers enviously regarded Umm ul'Banaat. The daughters all enviously regarded Jana. Umm ul'Banaat wafted *bukhoor* smoke in all of her daughters' faces before they left the house for the party.

"You can't be too careful as sisters of the woman with the good fortune of marrying BenAli," she said practically. She sprayed them with rose water, dug all of the horn, hand, and eye amulets she could find out of the bottom of her jewelry box and affixed them to any of her daughters who would stand still long enough to have one surreptitiously pinned to her attire, and had them all read the *mu'awidaat* into their hands and wipe their hands over their bodies afterwards. The latter was the only thing that Maryam participated in, of course, it being the sunnah means of protection against the evil eye. She threatened her mother that she would throw any gold amulets she found on her person into the garbage.

***

"Well, looks like we're officially sisters-in-law, of a sense," Kareema remarked, watching Jana and BenAli stroll around the masjid garden in private conversation, faces bright and happy.

"Yup," Elizza said, face distorted in a forced smile.

"But listen, we're going to have to think of something to tell people about Leedya's 'past.' We can't have that taunting our families forever. It's such a *fadihah*." Elizza's eyes narrowed.

"There's no *fadihah* at all. My sister is married to a good Muslim man. End of." She walked away sharply, regulating her breathing to calm her anger.

What a trial it was going to be to be connected to that woman, she thought. More so for Jana than for herself. Jana was too sweet to stand up for herself. Some people we so self-centered, it was hard to sympathize with them.

Elizza contented herself with declining to try. Instead, she pictured Kareema being punched in the face. *Ya Rabb*, she prayed, make it happen one day to humble her. Not me, of course, I would never want to be the one to cause friction between lovely Jana and her husband. But *Ya Rabb*, someday, please send someone to punch her in her smug face, with me as a witness, to satisfy my yearning to see her taught a lesson, that leads her to becoming a better, or less awful, person. *Ameen.*

Elizza hoped that she could develop more neutral feelings toward Kareema one day. One day, *insha'Allah*. But for now, she'd content herself with that *duaa*.

CHAPTER THIRTY

"I don't know if this is a good idea, Elizza. He did a dishonorable thing and now I just hand my daughter over to him?"

"They already did their *kitab*, Baba," Elizza reminded him, discussing Leedya and George. BenAli offered to share his and Jana's *walimah* party with the couple, and Umm ul'Banaat was adamant that her husband allow them to do so. "You promised her that when the semester started they could start living together with your blessing."

"They can get a quiet divorce without any fuss."

"They wanted to get married."

"We wanted someone better for her," he replied, sighing. "And I should just be happy they did their *kitab* so people stop gossiping about this?"

"I thought I would have this conversation with Mama," Elizza said with a small smile. "Not with you."

"I was born and raised in Libya, Elizza. I know I shouldn't mind, but it has been ingrained in me since infancy."

"I want to tell you that it doesn't matter what people think, but you already know that. But what is really most important isn't other people anyway. It's Leedya. She seems to be happy about everything. They were so desperate to marry each other they made cakes of themselves doing it. They made themselves out to be this Romeo and Juliet couple and just ran with it. It would be foolish to stand in the way."

"Leedya has always run headlong into life. I just thought she would slow down before she hit any real walls."

"In this case, it looks like she blasted through the wall. She's tougher than you think, Baba. Just give this marriage a chance. I know it's not your ideal, but try to thank Allah (SWT) that the situation didn't turn out worse than it did. At one point we were all wondering if Leedya had been kidnapped or run away from home to go live with some rando."

"I will try, *habibti*."

"So, they can hold their party with Jana?" Elizza wheedled. That was what she came in here for in the first place. She couldn't let that go. He sighed again.

"*Tafadaloo*," he said, irritably. "Everyone is welcome here. Let's celebrate all your relationships, past, present and future, get it all out of the way now." Elizza wasn't sure if that was permission, exactly, but they would run with it and deal with the consequences later.

***

"Hajja Khadijah called me today," Umm ul'Banaat told her daughters over dinner, sounding flattered. Hajja Khadijah never called her. "Tarseen is getting engaged, she says. To her daughter." Elizza's head whipped up at the mention of Tarseen, then plummeted at the end of that sentenced. Engaged? To his cousin? Leedya shot her a look of concern, but she evaded her gaze.

"Eww," Kawthar said. Leedya contemplated.

"No, I might marry a cousin," she decided. "Elizza almost did." She smirked. Kawthar snickered.

"It's like marrying your brother," Kawthar argued.

"Not like we would know the difference," Leedya replied. Elizza declined to think too carefully about that statement, too caught up with the news, trying to picture the cousin, and come to terms with a Tarseen out of reach.

"I mean, only if he was hot, obviously."

"It's not *haram*," Maryam said thoughtfully.

"Ugh," Kawthar said.

"And not annoying," Leedya continued. She never let interruptions stop her train of thought. "Which is a rare find in any man these days, let alone be so fortunate to have both in a cousin—so, unlikely, but I personally wouldn't rule it out."

"Let me phone Libya, then," Maryam quipped. "We've got some cousins who would like to escape to the land of opportunity—from the land of none."

"Too bad she's already taken," Kawthar said on a laugh.

"All the more reason," Maryam said under her breath.

"*Himara!*" Leedya said, backing out of her chair. Elizza snapped out of her stupor.

"You guys, grow up. And I can't believe you're married," she muttered at Leedya. "You're both giving me a migraine." Well, her sisters weren't helping it, anyway. It was easier to blame the pain on her sisters than the other news.

***

The thing about sharing a room with a sister, no matter how close, is that unless you wanted her, and the rest of your family, to be privy to all of your secrets and wishes and sadly squashed hopes, you couldn't just flop onto your bed and sob into your pillow when you suffered a disappointment, like you wanted to. You had to lay down quietly, stare at the ceiling and will the tears to stay safely hidden, capping their flow from your tear ducts until suppressing them exacerbated your pre-existing headache, until the physical pain gave you a real, legitimate and excusable reason to curl up into the fetal position, clutch your head when you really wanted to clutch your heart, and cry.

CHAPTER THIRTY-ONE

Elizza scarcely had time to nurse her broken heart. And since no one in the family knew about it, except Leedya, who didn't *really* know but harbored suspicions, no one was going to let her sit around miserably eating ice cream, watching romantic comedies while simultaneously abusing the males in them as liars, like she wanted to, and get out of helping her sisters get the decorations and their wardrobes in order.

Even though Jana was the real belle of the ball, as it was her husband actually paying for everything, Leedya took over everything. Including the selection of Jana's wedding dress.

"Uhh, no," she said the day they went to the only ready-made wedding dress shop in their town, "you are *not* wearing a ball gown. That is *so* ten years ago. You have to wear something tasteful. Think Kate Middleton."

"You can wear the lacy, classy concoction of your choice," Elizza spat. "Let Jana wear whatever makes her feel beautiful."

"You already *know* you're beautiful," Leedya said. "I want you to *be* beautiful. And your soft kind of beauty needs the dress of a princess… a real-life princess, not a Disney one." She held a sample out in front of her, then thrust it at Jana.

"See? Now go try it on." Jana resignedly hung the ball gown she was going to try on back up and disappeared into one of the large dressing rooms. Elizza rolled her eyes. "If you can't fight for your own choice of wedding dress I have no idea how you're going to survive marriage," she shouted. Jana declined to respond. She shrugged her shoulders. *Not my problem, not my problem*, Elizza thought. She was back on that mantra. If she said it enough times, maybe…the rest of her sisters would get married and it would come true. Sometimes she worried she would become just like her mother completely unconsciously and start scheming on behalf of Maryam and Kaw-thar. God save them all.

"Where's *your* princess gown?" Elizza asked Leedya, eyeing the dresses Leedya was lining up to try on herself.

"Oh, princess is not for me," she said confidently. Elizza laughed. Of course.

"Are you sabotaging Jana so you can look better?" she accused.

"Of course not!" Leedya said, truly offended. "I'd never do that. Anyway we have different kinds of beauty. I don't have the innocent face of a princess. I'm going for an understated sexy look."

"Ugh, save it for your lingerie," Elizza said. But then Leedya held out the dress she was the most excited about, a smooth cream crepe with a long train, baring her back all the way to the top of her hips, but a surprisingly modest neckline and long sleeved in the front, vine silver embroidery along the sleeves and the edges of the bodice. It was lovely.

"That's lovely," Elizza said softly. "Understated sexy. Got it. Go try it on." Leedya smiled. Her true, radiatingly lovely smile, not her fake Instagram one.

"What about you, Elizza?" she asked, her voice soft and affec-tionate.

"What about me?" Elizza shot her a challenging look. She did not want to be taken to task by her little sister.

"Won't you try some on? You know, for your own wedding. One day. So you know what you like."

"I'm good," she said, avoiding her sister's gaze. Leedya continued to stare.

"You haven't heard from…" she trailed off, still assessing Elizza.

"No, I haven't. I'm fine, Leedya. You're way off, so just… go try on that beautiful dress already."

"You can't just let him marry his cousin without… talking to him," Leedya said, unrelenting.

"Leedya, it's none of your business," she said, furious now. "And I don't care what he does."

"Elizza…."

"I'm done talking about this," she said, almost shrill now. She was also afraid she was perilously close to tears. Leedya probably sensed it too, because she let it go, picking up the dresses she had hanging up to try.

"You're always so busy worrying about us," she said before walking to the dressing room. "Just, don't forget that you're allowed to think about yourself sometimes."

***

After that conversation, Elizza avoided Leedya as much as she could, but felt somewhat bad doing so. Leedya would be moving away in a matter of weeks and she should be cherishing their remaining time as sisters living in the house of their childhood together. But she could not deal with dwelling on her feelings, so she avoided the only person who suspected them.

Soon, the wedding was all planned. Everyone had their outfits. Jana and BenAli still found time during the madness to get out together, now that they were Islamically allowed some alone time. So she had very little interaction with anyone in her family.

Except her uncle, who called her to let her know that she had a Libyan businessman seriously interested in investing in her business.

"*Akeed?*" she asked, incredulous. *For real?* Her uncle was totally serious. He asked her to send PDFs of her business plan again and sent her some copies of contracts to review.

"It's a partnership?"

"He's offering to be a silent investor," he said. "No management interests in the business, just purely given a percentage of the profits. His offer is very generous, actually, for what he is offering to initially invest. He must really see the potential of your ideas."

Elizza was floored, and excited. She agreed to send the papers back to the investor via her uncle by a date after the wedding. She did not have time to review anything before then.

So she threw herself into preparations. And during any free time she had, she did more research and tried to think about what her future would look like as a female business owner who owned a trans-Atlantic company.

***

"Uhh, was she invited?" Kawthar whispered to Elizza. She looked to the entrance of the hall to see Hajja Khadijah walk through the door, discarding her abaya and hijab into the dutifully open arms of her lovely daughter, fluffing up her coiffed short hair expertly before scanning the room for acquaintances.

"No," Elizza answered. She purposely omitted sending her one when she wrote out the invitations, even though her mother, still flattered by the phone call, insisted they include the *hajja* in their numbers. Elizza really wasn't in the mood to see her, or Anaya's lovely face. She watched Hajja Khadijah continue to scan the room before landing directly on her, heavily lined eyes seeming to shoot daggers. *What's with her?* Elizza looked away uncomfortably. Some people just had a propensity to hate everyone.

***

Elizza washed her hands, and looked into the bathroom mirror to smooth a smudge of runny mascara off of her eyelid. The door to the bathroom opened. Glancing at the door, she saw Hajja Khadijah walk through. *Time to go*, she thought, and stood up straight to grab a paper towel, making for the door.

"*Dageega*," the Hajja said. One minute. "*Bila alaik, shidili shanti.*" *If you would, hold my purse.* "I need to make wudhu." Elizza suppressed a sigh and took her ornately sequined gold purse, not bothering to mention that the bathroom stalls had hooks. The imperious were not to be reasoned with.

"This is a nice hall," the Hajja said, as she scrubbed her hands in the ritual for cleansing before prayer. "How much did it cost to rent?" People like her never hesitated to ask the price you paid for anything.

"A couple thousand, maybe," Elizza said, purposely vague. She didn't need to know the exact price, or that BenAli was footing the entire bill even though Leedya and George were also celebrating their kitab.

"Next time, ask me. I would have gotten a better deal," she said dismissively. Elizza doubted she would bother. She wished the Hajja would just finish already. She wanted to get away. Hajja

Khadijah's penetrating stares were making her feel claustrophobic.

"So your sisters are basically married," she went on. And then she went on the offensive. "No one asking about you yet?" Elizza just forced a smile, noting that the Hajja had only *just now* finished washing her face. Elizza tallied: hands, mouth, nose, *face*, arms, hair, ears, feet. "It's harder for you older ones to get married," she scoffed. "You all have too many opinions about everything. You've gotten used to your independence."

"That is the *fitnah* of our generation, for sure," Elizza said, ironically.

"You all want careers, and then you end up neglecting your children and your husbands and breaking your families apart."

"True, it's sad when families break apart," Elizza said, watching Hajja Khadijah scrub her ears as vigorously as she would if she were in the shower. After barely touching her perfectly styled hair, of course, Elizza noted in amusement. "Still," she couldn't help adding, "sometimes divorce can be a blessing."

"You American-raised girls can never make real Libyan men happy," the Hajja spat, seemingly out of nowhere. "Unless your mother spent considerable effort teaching you the proper *akhlaq*, and how to cook all the Libyan dishes and sweets, and memorizing the Qur'an, which I know for a fact yours hasn't, you girls wouldn't know the first thing about how to be good Libyan wives."

"And yet BenAli is marrying my sister," was all she could say. She was truly dumbfounded. *What is going on?*

"I'm not talking about her!" she almost screamed. "I mean you. But even your *haadiya* sister is biting off more than she can chew."

"Fortunately," Elizza said, trying to keep her voice calm, "the opinions of people like you don't make a difference in the matter. BenAli, and lots of other men with spines, have started choosing their own wives."

"You will never be welcome in my family," Hajja Khadijah said, finality in her voice. "You could never make him happy, and would be causing *gata'al arhaam* between his family and begin your marriage in a big sin. Just think about that." And with that, she pulled her foot out of the sink of the bathroom, slipped on her slightly high heeled shoe, and trounced out. Elizza stared at the door, rocking on its hinges from the force of the Hajja's slam. *Does she mean Tarseen?* Elizza wondered, staring at her reflection in the mirror, a thoughtful expression dawning on her face. *But, he's engaged.*

Isn't he?

CHAPTER THIRTY-TWO

The celebrations ended without a hitch. That entire period of time felt like a whirlwind to Elizza. She tried to enjoy it as much as possible—it was her family's first wedding, after all, and with someone else footing the bill and being generous with hiring help for setup and cleanup, she did not have as much to do as she may have had—might for her own wedding. Still, she was busy enough to have to tell herself to enjoy herself, to stop worrying about logistics and dance, to share her last moments with Jana all to herself before she moved away forever, to have serious discussions with Leedya (who steadily and staunchly avoided such discussions). The morning after breakfast she got through in a daze and buzz of activity, carrying the ingredients for *sphinz* and *aseeda* around for the Libyan matrons to prepare, picking up large jars of honey and date syrup from the Arabic store, and exclaiming in annoyance when Jana showed up to the house (a whole hour late) rosy cheeked and happy but not even dressed in the outfit she was supposed to be wearing and wearing absolutely no makeup, her hair hanging wild around her face as if fresh from the shower. Elizza rolled her eyes and made Leedya, who had actually shown up on time, attend to her before trying to ignore the knowing smiles and winks exchanged between the Libyan ladies who got a look at her sister before Elizza shuffled her away and up the stairs to their room.

It was impossible to find anything in the boxes that were sitting on top of Jana's bed, waiting to follow her to her new home. Elizza rummaged through them desperately for a few minutes before giving up and rummaging through the boxes on Leedya's bed. She had to take a few deep breaths not to dissolve into tears at the sight of them. She was so exhausted the day before she scarcely noticed the evidence of her sisters' departure from their home forever sitting there, taunting her.

It did not take her long to find a bedazzled kaftan to dress Jana in, and she carelessly plucked the clothing she had taken out of the boxes back into them before returning to the room. Leedya was just finishing Jana's look with a layer of mascara.

"Best I can do in five minutes," she was muttering. She hated to do anything haphazardly—especially when it had to do with one's looks. Elizza just shook her head in amusement.

"I thought I put your outfit in your night bag," she commented, confused.

"I'm not sure," Jana said dreamily. Leedya snorted.

"I'll leave you guys to it, then," Leedya said as she left the room. Jana and Elizza looked at each other, Jana somewhat distracted, Elizza's face wearing a wistful smile. Jana had difficulty tamping down her smile, even knowing that this was the beginning of her separation from her sister. Suddenly she stopped trying, unable to resist the happiness, a smile of such radiance and brilliance lighting up her face, practically making it glow. Elizza smiled back, but could not stop the trickling of a tear or two down her cheeks as she moved in to hug her sister.

"Jana, I'm so glad you're happy," she whispered. "I'm going to miss you."

***

The days after that drifted by as the rest of the family cleaned up the house post wedding celebrations and adapted to life without the oldest and youngest of the sisters. Elizza's leave taking of Leedya was less emotional. Leedya moved in to swipe Elizza into a quick hug before releasing her just as quickly, then chuckled at the look on Elizza's face.

"I'll be fine, don't worry so much," she said. "I am wiser to the ways of the world than you guys all assume." She looked on the verge of an eye roll.

"I know…" Elizza said. "Just…you're my little sister. I will always feel protective. If you ever need anything…"

"I *know*, Elizza," Leedya huffed. "Now some advice for you—try to be less judgmental of everyone." She turned around to leave, and

Elizza was left with a feeling of dissatisfaction that lingered with her for quite a while after that.

***

She looked at her sisters' possessions, the last of Jana's boxes that remained at their house. There were only a few of them left, so Jana said they would arrange for a shipping company to come pick them up sometime that day. They would not fit in the truck she drove away in with BenAli.

She roved her hands over the boxes, recalling memories from the possessions she could see peaking out of the tops. A corner of the belly dancing scarf they bought from the local bazaar, to wear to the few classes they'd attended together, Jana standing shyly in the corner, uncomfortable dancing in front of strangers. The female instructor, drawn to Jana's beauty, singling her out to her embarrassment to demonstrate some of the hand movements.

A piece of the jean pants the sisters all tried to share, like the travelling pants, that seemed to melt to fit whoever wore them (despite the 20 or so pounds of variation between all of their weights), leaving their home with Jana, who was the only one still nostalgic enough to want to wear the seven year old pair. Elizza had an urge to try them on, and took them out of the box to stuff her hips into the pants that seem to have shrunk a little with age. It probably didn't have anything to do with her form filling out into more womanly curves. She eyed her rear end critically. She didn't remember them making it look quite so round before.

She was startled out of her assessment by the sound of the doorbell. She waited a beat to hear who it was as someone else answered the door. But no one did. Her father was home. Her mother and sisters… she vaguely recalled that they had fled to the mall a few hours ago. She waited another second before groaning audibly. Her dad would be zoned out, so intensely reading the news about Libya that he probably didn't even hear the door. Either that or napping. Elizza took a look at the boxes she would probably have to haul down the stairs by herself and sighed, hastily pulling a long sweatshirt over her pants and wrapping a white scarf around her messily tied up hair.

"Coming," she sang down the stairs as she ran, and opened the door abruptly. Her heart thudded violently in her chest when she saw Tarseen standing on her front porch, hands shoved deeply into his pockets, staring at her, looking somewhat ill at ease.

Neither of them spoke. His dark eyes watched her face, absorbing her every expression. She had to remind herself to breathe.

"*Assalaamu'alaikum*," he said. "I was sent to pick up your sister's boxes to take with me on my way back. I think I will have enough room…" he said, trailing off. Then he looked up at her, hand travelling out of his pocket to sweep through his hair. His signature nervous gesture. And he laughed a nervous laugh.

"I'm sorry," he said, unnerved by her silence. "This is the second time I've lied to you about someone sending me on an errand I volunteered to do myself." She offered a small smile, her heart still thudding in her chest. It was so good to see him, but it also knifed her heart. *Is this our last meeting?* she wondered. She could barely take in any of his words, too distracted by her feelings. She tried to focus more on the present. To take in everything and cherish it.

"I *wanted* to come here," he said, holding her gaze. She blinked, confused.

"I'm glad you came," she said quietly. "So I could say, thank you for what you did. Or *Barak Allah feek.*" His face turned red.

"Just to thank me?" His voice sounded sad. "Well, what did I do?" he asked cautiously.

"For bringing Jana and your friend together again. And that other thing. With Leedya." Now it was her turn to blush.

"I couldn't live with myself knowing he still felt like I owed him something. Better lose money than have that against me on the Day of Judgment. He seemed to like your sister enough to cause all of that trouble so I hope I did the right thing. Money was the only obstacle he mentioned that was standing in the way of them getting married."

"You went overboard. We can't thank you enough." She glanced at him, then looked away again, noting his eyes still fixed on her face. It was suddenly all too much. Her sisters leaving, having to think about her own future, and maybe seeing Tarseen for the last time. She tried to school her expression to hide her sadness.

"Elizza," he said. His voice, the anguished sound of it, startled her so much that she did look into his face then. He glanced behind her into the house before continuing, taking an infinitesimal step closer. And just that much space disappearing between them robbed her completely of breath. "Please don't thank me," he continued. "I couldn't stand to see you so unhappy. That's why I really did it. Everything else was just..." he paused, "incidental." A small bubble of hope began to form somewhere in the region of her stomach. Her eyes roamed his face. Their gazes collided with almost visible force.

"Elizza," he repeated again. His voice was a low, pleading murmur. "I think we have gotten to know each other better now. We know so much more about each other than other people could even claim to know. So... do you think...have you changed how you feel... I mean, how you see me...at all? Enough to be able to chance building a life with me?"

She felt buoyant with happiness. Her face widened of its own accord into a brilliant smile. She was afraid of her physical response to his question, and felt the need to hug herself to keep herself from jumping out of the doorframe and hugging him. She tried to summon up an appropriate verbal response to his question, even as she saw an answering lightness and radiating happiness dawning on his face, in his solitary spot a few feet away from her on the porch. She opened her mouth to reply, before the sound of footsteps coming from behind her, and the sight of Tarseen's face clamming up into a neutral expression, chased away the already fluttering and uncaptureable pieces of coherent thought.

Elizza's father patted her shoulder from behind, smiling at her quizzically, then turning a welcoming face towards their guest.

"We have a visitor, Elizza?" he asked her. She turned around awkwardly, looking shyly away from her father's assessing gaze. But then she shrugged and shot Tarseen a coy look over her shoulder before responding to her father.

"Baba," she said, her smile wide, "Tarseen has something he wants to ask you." With that, she left them alone and raced upstairs to her room.

***

Elizza's father liked to speak in metaphors.

"Marriage," he said solemnly, after calling her down to his office to speak to her as soon as he saw Tarseen out, "is like a tree. A sapling, as it were. It needs nurturing. Patience. Kindness. It can eventually yield wonderful things. Can stand strong for years. Generations. But they're also very fragile in their tender years." He paused and examined her face, trying to assess whether she was following along. Elizza widened her eyes, a defense mechanism she developed over the years, mostly because that motion kept her from rolling them.

"Elizza," he continued, "we know that this tree will yield money. Lots of money," he emphasized, wincing. "But is it capable of providing shade? Will it be strong enough for others to lean on? Will it produce buds of spring after the frost of winter?" That sentence called to mind little buds, running around with their adorable Tarseen curls and Elizza's dark eyes, and she couldn't help but smile. Her father frowned.

"*Binti*, please," her father said. "Take this seriously for a moment." Elizza's smile melted. In all of her happiness, she had forgotten to consider the effect of her news on her father. She had an inkling that just the thought of her getting married made him feel intensely lonely. Her response needed to be careful and measured because of this—she just hoped she could find the words. She stayed silent a long while, the whole time her father noting and examining each expression as it materialized on her face.

"I don't know what to say, Baba, to show you that I am taking this seriously," she said, finally. "I think you know me better than to really suspect I'd make such a decision lightly. My sisters' recent experiences…" and yours, she wanted to say, but didn't, "all of them have shown me how important it is to choose with care. We've both sorely tried each other in lots of ways…" She faltered. She couldn't even describe what she meant, and that statement sounded like they had been dating or something. She wanted to cry, to run away from this awkward conversation, but she wouldn't leave her father in doubt that might plague him for a while after her marriage took place and be a cloud over it forever.

Suddenly, her father chuckled.

"Elizza, didn't you use to hate him?" Elizza just blushed. Her father laughed some more. "Doesn't his aunt dislike you?" Elizza just nodded resignedly. "You will have to watch out for those in-laws." With that, he patted her back and opened the door to allow her to escape.

***

The rest of her family's reactions were all different. Jana was incredulous.

"Are you serious?" she asked Elizza for perhaps the third time that phone call. Elizza sighed.

"Let me start from the beginning," she said, and told her sister the version of events she never had the courage to tell her before.

Her mother was dumbfounded.

"*Akeed*?" she asked--*Are you sure?*—echoing Jana's incredulity. It took her two days to get over the shock, and the feeling she was being pranked, but she rallied admirably...in the form of making boastful phone calls to all of their acquaintances about the good fortune of marrying not just *one*, but *two*, daughters off to wealthy men. But only after liberally steaming the house in incense and overtaking her husband's computer to play evil eye protection *duaa* on replay for several days, of course.

Maryam stared at her quietly for a few moments in contemplation, before finally saying, "You could do worse," and then enveloping her sister in a surprisingly fierce hug.

Leedya shouted a triumphant, "I knew it!" through the phone, before opportunely broaching another subject. "So, about the stipend amount. Do you think Tarseen could—?"

And finally, Kawthar, who chuckled softly, before a brooding expression overtook her face as the reality of being left at home with only Maryam and their mother for female companions finally sunk in.

"Ugh," she muttered. "I need to get married."

CHAPTER THIRTY-THREE

Elizza was a tumble of predominantly positive emotions, with a few neutral ones like nervousness and anxiety thrown in. She looked forward to her next meeting with Tarseen—which happened a few days after he came to pick up Jana's stuff, in the form of a chaperoned walk in the park (her sisters trailing out of hearing distance behind them)—with a mixture of excitement and anxiety that some things were too good to be true.

When he climbed out of his car upon seeing her arrive with her sisters, the change in his resting expression was startling. He wore a serene, calm and affectionate expression that completely altered his face, warring with the tense, brooding look he usually wore on other occasions. An expression, it seemed, that he wore just because of her. He waited for her to get out of the car before starting down the path at a gentle, leisurely pace, slowly closing the distance between them as they walked side by side down the path, still too shy with each other to make much eye contact.

"So I just want to get one thing out of the way first, before we make this *official* official. I take it you're not engaged to your cousin? Since you're getting engaged to me?" She smiled to indicate the joke, but eagerly—and a little anxiously, if she was honest—awaited his answer.

"What? What made you think—" then he stopped. "My aunt," he said shortly. She nodded, watching his face carefully. He looked angry for a moment, but then looked at Elizza's face, and stopped walking in an effort to get her to look at his. She glanced at her sisters down the path. They stopped, too, uncertainly, and looked at each other before avoiding looking at their sister and pretending to admire the surrounding garden of wildflowers. *Some chaperones they were*, Elizza thought in amusement.

"No, Elizza," he said softly. "I'm not. I need to have a talk with my aunt. And I don't think I'd be great at the two-wives thing..." he stopped to look at her earnestly, "especially since there is only one woman that I want." Elizza blushed and looked away before he did. Eventually he started walking again along the path, and they discussed other things. They talked about what sort of partnership they wanted in their marriage, how many kids they wanted, and when they would hold the wedding—"As soon as possible," Tarseen ventured with a wink—focusing on the future, until they were comfortable enough with each other to delve into the past. They discussed Jana and BenAli, and wore mirrored smiles as they amused themselves imagining the genial marriage they would have with their easygoing personalities. And then Elizza wondered aloud how Leedya was getting along with her marriage—she had not heard from her for a few days. Tarseen ventured some platitude about how she would probably be fine.

"How did you find them?" she asked curiously. Leedya and George had both disappeared as completely off of social media as they had physically. There was no trace of them that Elizza was capable of following.

Tarseen smiled sheepishly. "I hired a private investigator. He pretended to be an admissions officer contacting him about a scholarship. He wasn't too happy to be meeting with me instead of a school employee offering him money." He paused thoughtfully. "He seemed rather desperate at the time. Was sort of waiting for someone to pop out of the closet and say 'got you!' like he couldn't even trust his own luck."

They continued to walk, both lost in thought.

"What's wrong?" Tarseen asked, noticing her silence.

"I'm just thinking about this Leedya situation," she said, then explained the argument that caused their distance at the time. "I messed up royally with her. I was just trying to veer her in another direction, help her think about a way to move past it once she got tired of her hobby. Invest in something. Maybe I shouldn't have told her what I thought about her tutorials. It's not like I am so sure about my own takes on things. Well, not anymore," she added.

"Something new to invest in?" He said, "Oh, you wanted her to use her money to invest in your project so you could make it a reality."

"Oh yeah, I was after her $10,000 a year to find my project with the 5-million-dollar price tag."

"Is that all she makes?"

"I really have no idea," she laughed. "She never did let me help her sort out the business side of things."

"Well," he said after a thoughtful pause. "Your judgment was pretty spot-on about her going to that convention without your family."

"Yeah, that was a pretty clear train wreck waiting to happen."

"So trust yourself more. Doesn't mean you always have the answers, but there's nothing wrong with giving people your own opinion about what you think is right, even if you know they will disagree with you." Elizza smiled.

"I'll remember that then next time I don't agree with you."

"I didn't mean with me!" he said with a laugh. "No, I'm kidding. Of course. We will be partners. Doesn't mean you're going to win the argument so you can let me know what you think all you want." Elizza swatted his arm.

"Okay we'll go 50-50 then. But, if I recall correctly... you won our last argument so I think I'm due the next win. I'm just saying."

"I don't remember being the winner!" she laughed, turning to look at him. The smile dropped off of his face as they locked eyes.

"What did you think of me?" Tarseen asked curiously, intense eyes watching her face. "I mean, before you were convinced I was a terrible person. Or after you determined I wasn't?" Elizza paused for some minutes, shooting him a mysterious smile as her mind whirled, trying both to remember and to tactfully convey her thoughts.

"I think I was too worried about you disapproving of me to really think about you," she said finally. His face fell slightly and she laughed.

"But after we argued, and you emailed, my mind was never free of wondering about you. I wondered what kind of man you were, what could have possibly made you like me so much, if our argument made you unlike me, and if you were worth all of the brainpower I was using up on you." She paused. "What about you?" she asked shyly.

"You're a treasure," Tarseen said, turning to look at her. "I knew it as soon as I saw you." Elizza blushed.

"During that first look, you mean?"

"Must have been. I only had the one, after all." He winked. "I know this isn't very flattering, but I really couldn't figure out why at the time. But the more I get to know you, the more amazing things I discover about you."

"After you found out all the bad things, of course. I guess you just needed to balance out my seeming perfection to see me more clearly." He just smiled. Perhaps he could sense how uncomfortable his expressions of affection were making her. For a girl used to suppressing such stuff as improper outside of marriage, she felt like she needed time to get used to everything before letting her guard down and completely letting go.

CHAPTER THIRTY-FOUR

"**H**e's not coming in?" Leedya asked incredulously.

"Weird," Kawthar piped in.

"It's not weird. He's trying to be respectful to the ladies here. And to our religion. And for goodness sake, it's not the wedding it's just the *kitab*."

"Good for him," Maryam said.

"What a waste of your perfect hairdo," Leedya said. Elizza rolled her eyes, but smiled. She was starting to miss her sister's insults.

***

"Elizza, I just got a text from Kamal," Shayla said, a while later. "The guys need a *darbooka*." Elizza laughed.

"Seriously? They didn't remember from last time?" She picked up the one they had sitting against a side table. "Can you take it there real quick?"

"I, uhh. Your mom wants me to start serving tea," she said apologetically. "And we need that one," she added, snatching it. "There's a spare in the store room."

Elizza looked around to ask someone else but all her sisters were otherwise occupied. She sighed and made her way to the back to find it.

She opened the door to pitch black. She blindly felt for the light switch, but before she could make contact a flame appeared before her eyes, followed by another one, and then several more, candlelight suddenly illuminating the room. Tarseen's face loomed before her. She stopped short, shy and unprepared, her hands patting her uncovered hair, conscious of revealing it to the first nonrelative male ever. And hopefully the last, she silently prayed, as she took in his expression, heart pumping, racing, breath short. Taking in the sight of her handsome husband, his cream Libyan suit setting off his handsome olive skin to perfection.

He looked at her. His expression so many things she couldn't describe them all. An oxymoron of facial expressions—fierce but gentle, nervous, but exuberantly happy. They looked at each other, and simultaneously burst out in soft laughter. But then Tarseen, his expression turning suddenly serious again, whispered, "As beautiful on the outside as you are on the inside. You are breathtaking."

Epilogue

The Libyan fall is a subtle creature, intruding almost unnoticed into the lives of Libyan residents. The weather is barely distinguishable from summer, the social life just as busy. Perhaps freer in some respects, as the mothers' days are somewhat freed up by their little ones away at school for the bulk of the day. The temperature grows colder one tiny degree per week, and the days shorten and the nights lengthen bit by aching bit until winter hits and the warm clothing boxes are opened and checked for insect damage and the tones of people's voices modulate to accommodate the hums of the heaters that thrum during waking hours in the family room (*marbooah*) of the average Libyan house.

Elizza sits in the courtyard of a Libyan family's house, quietly watching the sunset approach, sipping *kakawiyah* next to a mother and her toddling boy, a cooling breeze ruffling the edges of her hijab. She sends the mother a warm smile, before letting her gaze drift to the figure of her husband, sitting with the Libyan father on the other side, teaching him how to operate the solar energy system they just helped the family install in their home, a system that will keep them in water, heat and electricity for the winter, and many years to come. Their gazes lock, and his conversation comes to a halt, as they savor the realization of their unified dream, and the culmination of that second look.